Jaime —

Thanks ~

CATHY MORRISON

Say Something

Together we make a difference.

Cathy Morrison

Stories Matter Publishing

First published by Stories Matter Publishing 2019

Copyright © 2019 by Cathy Morrison

Cover design by Tenaya Jayne

First published in 2019 by Cold Fire Publishing

First edition

ISBN: ISBN-13: 978-1-7341269-1-4

This book was professionally typeset on Reedsy.
Find out more at reedsy.com

To the women who were brave enough, caring enough, and strong enough
to share their stories with me. You know who you are.

If this book changes someone's life for the better, that's all you.

Thank you.

Dear readers,

Many survivors, members of law enforcement, and counselors
shared their experiences and challenges with me.

However, Maggie, the focus of this novel, is a fictional character.

This story is uniquely hers, and yet her story and her power belong to every survivor.

Say Something

Contents

II   Resources

I

The Story

Prologue

"Goodnight, Warren."

The little girl heard Mommy's quiet words as they drifted around the edges of her closed bedroom door.

Warren was spending the night. Again.

She clutched her favorite bear tight in her arms and thought about what to wear for the second day of first grade.

Warren's voice rumbled from somewhere in the house.

She stroked the soft bear, until her hand came to rest on his little paw. She worried the pad between her thumb and pointer finger. She'd wear the pink stretchy shirt with the silver sparkly cat on the front. She'd counted every one of the fifty-four pretty, silver sparkles the day Mommy bought it. Not everyone in her class could count to fifty-four. Yep, her favorite pink shirt and her new blue shorts.

Footsteps sounded in the hall, and she shut her eyes tight. The steps faded away.

And the purple and pink tennis shoes. They had silver sparkles, too. She opened her eyes and tried to see out the tiny crack in the blinds. Sometimes she imagined she could slip through the little space and fly away. Like a bird or a magic fairy.

She squeezed the bear's little paw tight as she rubbed the fur.

3

The door cracked open, but no light entered. Her eyes snapped shut again. A tremor ran along her body. The door closed quietly, and she heard breathing and footsteps muted by carpet. She smelled something spicy. The smelly stuff mommy's boyfriend wore.

Mommy said they were going to move into his fancy house where he'd made a princess room just for her.

She hated him.

The bed sagged, and when he scooted next to her, the warmth from his body creeped into her space. She lay very, very still.

"Hey there," he whispered, smelling like spicy stuff and beer. "How's my little beauty?"

Chapter One

"Who are you?" the girl asked.

Her blue eyes stared into mine, wide, innocent. Everyone thought she was so nice. Girl next door. But I knew the truth.

"Who are you?" she repeated.

Damn her. *I am who I am*, I thought and refused to answer. I wanted to look away, but her gaze narrowed, trapping me in the small space. Why the hell wouldn't she leave me alone?

I am who I am. We don't need to frickin' analyze it.

"Who are you?" she demanded.

I clenched my fist in frustration, then slowly, deliberately relaxed it and tucked a strand of hair behind my ear, as if her question meant nothing to me.

She mocked me with a similar movement.

The only way to shut her up was to answer. I knew it. I didn't like it, but I knew it.

"I'm Maggie."

She frowned, her eyes still boring into me, as if she could see into my brain. Into my soul. I disliked her misty blue eyes. What people called her *honey brown* hair. Her stupid girl-next-door looks. Her pretentious letter jacket. I should walk away. Yeah, that's what...

"I'm a good student," I blurted. Ah hell, now I'd engaged.

She raised her brows, clearly finding my answer insufficient. "I'm an athlete."

Nothing.

"I don't do drugs."

She shook her head in another mockery of my own movements. "Not what are you. *Who*. Who are you?"

Anger bubbled inside me, threatening to explode. If I didn't answer, I'd never get out of here. "I'm a survivor," I hissed.

Anger faded from her features, and sadness settled on her face. I preferred her judgement to this pity.

"Screw you," I told the mirror and spun around to rush out the door. If I didn't hurry, I was going to be late for class.

Who am I?

I had no damn idea.

Chapter Two

I used to love the color pink, until I found out pink is the color for little beauties.
   —Maggie's Journal

I should have stayed home today.

Thanks to my early morning discussion with mirror-me, I was almost late for first hour. And I hate being late. Especially on a day when I should have just stayed home.

Just pretend you're sick, I'd told myself. After all, I never missed school. Didn't I deserve to skip this one crappy day? Hadn't I earned it?

But no, the me in the mirror had driven me from my own home.

And now here I sat, in my last class, drawn to today's lecture like some stupid gawker to a car wreck.

Trying desperately to appear normal. As though today was just another regular day in health class.

"Be wary of people you meet online. Just because someone says he's a teenage boy or she's a teenage girl, doesn't mean they are." Ms. Williams, the new health teacher, paused.

I fought the urge to bang my head on my desk. She was making it worse by encouraging discussion.

Hands shot up around the room. Ms. Williams smiled. She didn't get it. Better to charge straight through the topic and be done with it. But she was, well, new. And nice.

And naïve.

"Yea, yea, yea, we know. It's not a teenager, it's a creeper." Kelvin, the defensive line superstar, spoke without being called on. He rolled his wrist, making small circles in the air, indicating Ms. Williams should speed things up.

His buddies snickered.

"We hear this e-v-e-r-y year," a guy near the window drawled.

"There are creepers online. Beware." Kelvin squinted down his nose and offered an exaggerated impersonation of a teacher. His ridiculous face caused everyone to laugh. Well, almost everyone.

At six-foot-five and all muscle, he was a tall, broad-shouldered, ebony-skinned force of nature. And the biggest jerk in our class.

Anger stirred inside me. I curled my toes in my boots and forced myself to relax. To appear normal, undisturbed by obnoxious behavior the rest of the class found amusing. I was the poster girl for *fake it 'til you make it*. Yep. That was me. I faked normal every day. I just hadn't made it yet.

I glanced at the clock. Still twenty minutes to go, but I'd already had enough. I wanted to bail, and yet...*car wreck in progress*.

Ms. Williams frowned in an attempt to stop the dumb comments. "The smartest approach is to just friend people you know."

How had I, Maggie Bryant, regular girl, gotten stuck in this class full of the most annoying members of the popular crowd? I bit the inside of my lip. I really wished I'd stayed home.

The cheerleader, Brandi, who sat in the middle toward the back of the room, exhaled an exaggerated sigh, signaling disinterest. She caught me watching her. We stared, gazes locked, and then...she winked.

I smiled and almost meant it. There were days when I thought it would be so much easier to be like her. Uninhibited, free. Instead of me.

Ms. Williams pressed the clicker, and a new slide appeared on the smart board.

CHILD MOLESTERS.

My heart skipped a beat.

Child molesters. Pedophiles. Perverts.

Slouching in my chair, I observed the others. They mostly seemed embarrassed or bored, ready for the school day to end.

"Just because you're teenagers doesn't mean you're safe from predators." Ms. Williams forged ahead.

Predators. Forgot that one.

"Yea, well, if anyone tried anything with me, I'd kick him in the nuts so hard he wouldn't bother anyone ever again." Laughter followed this comment from the jerk near the windows.

Matt McGuire punched douche bag on the arm, muttering, "Shut up." As popular athletes go, he fell into the less annoying category. And he was so cute that I almost regretted self-selecting out of the popular crowd freshman year.

He glanced my way—crap!—and caught me staring. My gaze sliced back to Ms. Williams in what I hoped was a calm, I-wasn't-watching-you way, and I pretended heat wasn't creeping up my cheeks.

9

Yeah, he was cute and not a jerk.

We'd been lab partners the previous year, and I still had his number in my phone. He was smart, did his fair share of the work. And we might have flirted a little.

Sometimes I felt him watching me, and it didn't feel creepy. But I didn't date, so it didn't matter.

I forced myself to focus on Mrs. Williams' lecture. In her first year of teaching, she sometimes struggled with the idiots in our class. Impressed that she kept trying, I sat up straighter, showing quiet support even as my gaze was drawn back to the others.

Most of them were so *ignorant*.

"I know you think this won't happen to you. That it doesn't happen in your school, in your neighborhood." Ms. Williams scanned the room, catching the eye of as many students as possible. "But statistics tell us that one in four girls and one in six boys will be sexually abused before the age of eighteen."

I glanced around the room. The Hispanic girl, Elena, in the third row by the window, studious with long straight black hair. Quiet but smart, she was shy and avoided social situations even more than I did. With a little makeup and less frumpy clothes, she'd be gorgeous.

Next, cheerleader Brandi with her expensive clothes and a new boyfriend each month. She was rich and beautiful, and everyone knew it.

And finally, the painfully shy boy in the back row. Mike. His strawberry blond hair looked like he cut it himself. Every day he wore jeans, a black T-shirt, and canvas high tops. He'd moved to the school this year. I'd never heard him utter more than a few words.

Elena, Brandi, and Mike. All victims of sexual abuse, I'd bet on it. It was in their eyes, in their body language. Subtle, but there.

Ms. Williams continued to lecture. *How to identify sexual predators.* This *how* was easy when you were being abused—you knew the predator. *How to report.* Call the hotline. *Duh.*

But what about the *if* and *when*? I clenched my fists in my lap, and then forced them to relax, not wanting to betray my frustration. Sure, *make the call* sounded easy. But what about the *consequences* of reporting? The annual lecture never dealt with the fallout. Who would be hurt emotionally? Who would be in physical danger?

The bell rang, and I breathed deep, glad to be free of this class. Normally I liked Ms. Williams. But today? Not so much.

I plopped my bag on my desk and stood, Elena, Brandi, and Mike still circling my thoughts.

I could always tell who the victims were.

And I wondered—if I recognized other survivors of sexual abuse, how many of them recognized me?

Chapter Three

Most days I wear a mask.
—Maggie's Journal

I shoved the books into my backpack as memories crowded my head. This is why I should have skipped school. The class was annoying, but it was the unwanted memories that really sucked.

Mom dancing into my room in our little rented house when I was eight, telling me Warren would change our lives. I'm sure she'd meant for the better.

Moving into his fancy, two-story Victorian house after he and Mom got engaged. A room just for me, all pink and frilly—a little girl's dream princess room.

A dull thud-thud-thud kicked in just behind my temples, and my stomach heaved, leaving me ill and shaky. I curled my toes tight in my boots. Released them, curled them again.

That memory receded.

My fourteenth birthday, Mom insisting on a mother-daughter lunch and a movie. A spinach salad with chicken, strawberries, and pecans.

Over three years later, I still hated the sickly sweet smell of raspberry vinaigrette.

A medium height, slim-shouldered man entering the restaurant with a small group, wearing a dark suit and red tie, tilting his head, smirking.

My heart pounding in my chest like the time a huge snake slithered across the path right in front of me.

Fear.

The man approaching our table with his wavy black hair and bright green eyes, chatting with everyone as he slowly made his way to us.

Mom gasping when I whispered, "Mom, who is that?"

Warren.

Warren.

The man—Warren—reaching our table and greeting my mom, "Tina, so good to see you." Then staring at me with his piercing eyes, smiling. "Look at you, Maggie, so grown up. You were quite the little beauty as a girl. Now you've become a lovely young woman."

The words little beauty rebounding inside my head, then plummeting into my stomach. My delicious salad churning in protest.

Discovering that a snake had in fact entered the restaurant.

* * *

"Hey, Maggie." Matt's friendly voice intruded on my ugly memories.

Startled, I shook off the shadows and pasted a friendly expression on my face, pretending I hadn't been caught standing zoned-out at my desk—like an idiot.

"Hey," I quipped, undoubtedly impressing him with my witty conversational skills.

13

Matt, starting offensive lineman for the state champion football team, smiled down at me. My unreliable heart, which had skipped a beat earlier, sped up without warning. My cheeks grew uncomfortably warm. He was tall. Although I was no shorty at five-foot-eight, I tilted my head back to meet his gaze.

He had skin that looked tanned every season of the year and gorgeous brown eyes. They regarded me without shadows, without lies, without fear. The eyes of someone who'd lived a nice, safe life. Spoiled but not obnoxious.

One of the popular people in class who hardly ever annoyed me.

Cute.

Normal.

"A group of us are going to the lake on Saturday for a cook out." He grinned. "Should be fun. Want to join us?"

Wow. One of the nicest and best-looking guys in our senior class had just asked me to join him—and his friends—at the lake. Completely unexpected...except I *had* felt him watching me. And, yeah, it felt nice. But that didn't matter. I opened my mouth to decline...and hesitated.

Who are you? A voice whispered in my head.

At age seventeen, I'd spent years avoiding relationships. I didn't date, didn't go to parties. I had acquaintance-friends but no close I-can-tell-you-anything BFF. Heck, except for sports, I'd spent most of my life avoiding involvement of any kind.

I was an island.

All because of *him*. Warren.

"Uh, Maggie?"

I blinked. Matt wore a perplexed expression on his handsome face. Great. He probably already regretted inviting me.

14

"It's no big deal, but if you want to join us…" His voice trailed off. One of his friends hollered from the doorway for him to hurry up. And still he waited.

Waited while I battled for control of my emotions. I looked into his friendly, if confused eyes, pissed that Warren still had so much influence over my choices. Yesterday, if Matt had asked, I'm pretty sure I would have said no. Not because I didn't like him. But because I didn't date.

But today? Today, I wasn't fully in control. I was angry, and my self-imposed boundaries were wavering. Why shouldn't I date? Before I could think it through, I forced a smile. "Sure. It sounds like fun."

My shrink would have been proud. Except that I said yes not only because I liked Matt but also because I hated Warren.

Panic bubbled in my throat. I brushed past Matt with a rushed, "Late for volleyball warm up. Uh, see you Saturday." Of course, I'd also see him tomorrow and Friday at school.

Smooth, Maggie.

Hurrying down the hall, I tugged a band from my wrist and pulled my hair into a ponytail. I should have been excited about tonight's game. Or excited about my date. It had been a date, right? Not just an invitation to hang out with the group?

I should have been excited. However, instead of *want to join us* replaying thrillingly, joyfully, nervously inside my head, the words *little beauty* ricocheted harshly, and the spicy scent of memory invaded my nostrils.

Feeling a little bit stupid and a lot of bit stressed, I hustled down the hall and into the girls' locker room.

"Hey, Maggie," our team captain greeted me.

I liked Aubree. She kept her cool under pressure, kept her grades up, and she was nice. The kind of person I might have

15

been friends with if my life had been different.

We were volleyball friends but not close friends.

"Hey." I spun my combination and whipped my locker open.

"You okay?" a new voice asked. Mari's voice. Mari was the reason I didn't have close friends. But she still cared, and it hurt.

"Huh?" I looked up and found not one, not two, but five concerned faces turned my way. The varsity starters. I peeked into my little locker mirror.

Crap. My cheeks were flushed, eyes distracted. I looked...disturbed. Awesome.

"Yeah, sure, I'm fine. Just running late." I forced a smile.

"Okay, see you on the court." Aubree thunked my shoulder. "Don't be late."

They left the locker room, talking and laughing. Except for Mari. I felt her worried glance before she gave up and trailed after them. Sometimes I felt her watching me, and while it also didn't feel creepy, it made me feel...guilty.

I dressed in record time and joined the team with seconds to spare before warmups. Thank goodness, because Coach didn't like slackers. And in her mind, tardy equaled slacker.

Tonight varsity scrimmaged JV, and I was glad. I tried to focus on the game.

We're going to the lake.

I dove and made a perfect pancake save.

"Want to join us?"

"No."

I jumped high. Spike!

"Yes. I mean yes."

What should I wear?

Little beauty.

16

Excitement and nightmares and daydreams warred for control of my thoughts, with Warren creeping up on all that was good about my day.

"What do you want, Warren?" Mom asked the man I barely remembered.

He stared. "I just wanted to say hi."

The corners of his eyes crinkled, and he nodded. "Good to see you, Maggie."

"Maggie, it's your serve.

Crap. And thank God. I loved serving. The serve was either good or bad. I controlled the serve.

I tossed the ball and—whack!—I slammed it across the net.

Warren left our table, but the faint scent of spice lingered, unpleasant and disturbing. Tiny hammers pounded inside my head.

I served again. Ace!

I frowned at Mom. "I'm glad you got rid of that guy. He's kind of, I don't know...creepy." I shrugged.

Tossing the ball high, I leapt into the air and slammed it across the net.

Ace!

Mom fluttered her hands. "Yes, well, he wasn't one of my better choices."

I channeled all of the crap into each serve. Again. And again. And again.

Eight serves straight, three aces. Game and match. We headed for the locker room.

"You were on fire tonight." Aubree clapped me on the back.

I grinned. I *had* been pretty amazing.

"Sometimes you get in a zone, and it's like *wow*. I wish I had that."

My grin faded. *No, you don't.* "Thanks. Just a lucky night."

I took my time in the shower, hoping they'd be gone, but Aubree and Mari were waiting.

"Want to go for yogurt with us?" Aubree asked, hair still damp.

Mari waited silently beside her. I hesitated, remembering the Mari of my youth. She would have butted right in with *of course she's coming.* That was before I pushed her away for good.

"No, thanks. I've got to study."

Aubree paused. "Well, okay."

I always said no.

Always.

Because yogurt lead to talking.

Talking led to sharing.

And eventually, the effort to maintain my distance became too much.

I refused to let anyone close enough to share the truth.

The last time I told the truth, I'd lost a friend. Mari. I still carried that loss inside me like a rock. Even after all these years.

But sometimes I thought maybe...maybe I'd join them.

Just not tonight.

By the time I arrived home, finished studying, and crawled into bed, the night of my fourteenth birthday had crept back into my mind. The night after Warren intruded on my special day, bursting front and center back into my life.

That night I'd crawled into bed in our modest, three-bedroom ranch, in the small Summit Heights subdivision. The place we'd lived ever since Mom split with Warren.

I'd crawled into bed that night not exactly innocent of the

evil of the world, but ignorant of its place in my life.

A little after midnight, I'd awoken in a cold sweat, my heart pounding, blankets clutched in clawed hands.

Happy fourteenth birthday, Maggie.

The night terrors had begun.

Chapter Four

Maggie, age 8

"If someone touches you where your swimsuit goes, or touches you and it feels bad or confusing, what should you do?"

Wide-eyed, twenty-four kids chanted, "Tell a trusted adult." One of the boys giggled. They thought it was a game.

Maggie sat very still, certain she was the only one who knew this wasn't a game.

The only one who had ever been touched in a bad way in a private place.

The bell rang, and kids scrambled to be first in line for lunch. Maggie moved slowly, her mind on the counselor's words. *Tell a trusted adult.* She wished she could.

"Maggie, come on!" Mari waved her forward. She hated to be at the end of the line.

Grabbing Maggie by the arm, her best friend rushed them through the hall, managing to land them in the middle of the line despite their late start. Ms. Hollis frowned at them, but Mari smiled and tucked her hair behind her ear, pretending innocence, and Ms. Hollis smiled back. They filed into the cafeteria.

Mari had the best silky black hair. Maggie thought she

looked like a princess.

Maggie and Mari sat at the end of a table. Maggie stirred her mashed potatoes with her spoon, blending them with the runny gravy until a pile of light brown mush covered her plate.

"Are you going to eat that?" Mari pointed to her chocolate chip cookie.

Maggie shook her head. Mari snatched it off her plate.

"That's weird, huh? The touching? What would you do if that happened? Who would you tell? I'd tell my mom." Mari took a big bite of cookie.

Peeking down the length of the table, Maggie thought some of the other kids heard the question. She shrugged.

Before Mari could question her further, Ms. Hollis gave the sign to line up. Their class went directly from lunch to recess, and so, five minutes later, Maggie found herself in a corner of the playground with Mari, thinking about telling a trusted *person*—maybe not an adult, but the person she trusted most in the world. Mari. As she debated her options, Mari dove back into the conversation.

"So, I'd tell my mom or maybe Ms. Hollis. Who would you tell?"

A lump formed in Maggie's throat. "I dunno. It's not that easy."

"Sure it is. 'Mom, we gotta talk.'" Mari used her best grown up voice.

"It's not that easy," Maggie insisted, frustrated. When Mari opened her mouth to argue, she added, "Mariko." Mari's mom called her Mariko when she was serious.

Her eyes widened, and she twirled a strand of her shiny black hair around her finger, frowning. "How do you know?"

Mari thought she knew everything, but this time only

Maggie knew the truth. She blurted it in a quiet voice, "I know because Mommy's boyfriend touches me."

Mari froze, and her mouth dropped open. She stared at Maggie's face as she leaned forward and whispered, "Like, where your swimsuit goes?"

Maggie nodded, relieved to have told someone the truth at last. Mari reached out and took her hand. *Now what?* She glanced at the sky, then the ground, then the tree near the school, as she wondered what to say next. A friend called them over to swing. They jogged to join her, still holding hands, and Maggie was relieved Mari hadn't asked more questions.

At the end of the day, they hugged, repeating the same thing they said every day, "See you tomorrow, *tomodachi.*" *Friend.*

Even though she knew there was nothing a kid could do, Maggie still felt somehow lighter for having told.

* * *

Maggie was called into the counselor's office the next morning.

Only kids in trouble got called to the office, unless there was testing. When a teacher's aide sat with the class while Ms. Hollis walked with Maggie, she chewed her bottom lip, trying to think what she'd done wrong.

When the door opened, Maggie shuffled in. Ms. Hollis crouched down in front of her. "Maggie, you're not in trouble. We're going to help you."

They sat at the little round table with the counselor. Ms. Hollis held Maggie's hand. "Mari told her mom what you said about your mom's boyfriend, and she called me. In a minute, we're going to go talk to a really nice lady from Children's Services."

Maggie frowned. Children's Services didn't sound nice. It sounded icky, like going to the dentist.

There was a knock at the door. Ms. Hollis gave her a hug and left. The counselor took her hand, and they entered the principal's office.

The principal wasn't alone. There was a lady from the place called Children's Services. She smiled, and Maggie relaxed a little. She looked nice.

But then Maggie heard a sniffle and turned. Mommy was in the room. Her eyes were red. And her nose. She didn't even say hello. Just sat there and cried, the great big kind of tears that Maggie hated.

That's how she knew she was in big trouble after all.

Chapter Five

The first time I told someone, I was in second grade. The school counselor came to class and talked about bad touching. She said if bad touching happened to you, you should tell a trusted adult.

It's funny how years later and after I'd completely blocked everything, I now remember this class so clearly.
  —Maggie's Journal

Friday arrived. Important because it was the day before Saturday. And Saturday was B-Day.

Bonfire Day.

Boy Day.

Maggie's Bigtime Brave Day.

The seventh hour bell rang. Students continued talking, focused on their weekend plans. Ms. Williams ignored us all, strolling casually around the room, dropping a piece of paper on each desk.

When she finished, she returned to the front of the class and waited. Conversations gradually slowed.

Almost a full minute passed before all of the chatter stopped.

I examined the piece of paper in my hand. *14.* Great. The year I battled night terrors. One of my *unlucky* numbers.

"What's up?" Kelvin asked. He held his piece of paper in the air. "If you're giving me a number, eight ain't it. More like *numero uno*." He puffed up.

Ms. Williams smiled at him. Just what the guy needed. Encouragement.

"Well, Kelvin, you—and the rest of the class—didn't take Wednesday's material very seriously."

Groans sounded around the room.

"So today we're going to do something a little different."

"Whatever happened to recess? That's good for our health." Someone grumbled from the back.

She ignored the comment. "Numbers one through four stand up." Four students stood across the room. She hadn't handed the numbers out in any kind of order that I could tell. A few folks whispered.

"Sit down."

Everyone sat.

"Numbers five through ten stand up." This time six students stood. "Sit."

"Numbers eleven through sixteen."

And so it continued until everyone in the class had stood as part of a group of four, five or six. By the end no one spoke.

I began to understand.

Ms. Williams paused, then called a non-sequential set of numbers. Two, twenty-six, eighteen, and ten. As each group stood, the members cast increasingly uncomfortable glances at each other. Their gazes cut to those seated and back to Ms. Williams. When the next group was called, those standing slid into their seats, some thoughtful, some annoyed, some confused. Again and again, she called numbers until each person had stood as part of a group.

When the last group sat, silence reigned, shifting bodies creating the only sound in the room.

She had everyone's attention.

Brandi spoke first. "You're saying each time we stood up, based on statistics, one person in the group has been abused." She strived for a flip I-get-it-and-it-bores-me, but an undercurrent of somberness ruined the effect.

It surprised me—not that she went first or her tone, but the quality of her insight.

"Or that any one group could represent everyone in the class who's been abused," Brandi continued.

"Way to kill the Friday mood, Ms. Williams," a guy near the window added.

"Turn to page 115 in your book. Today we're discussing..."

"So what's the point?" someone behind me called.

My heart thudded in my chest. The point? Take it seriously. *It could be you*, I wanted to say, but the words remained deep inside me.

I searched the room. Being an island had honed my observation skills, one small perk of living life on the sidelines. My heart calmed. Understanding stood out on every face. It appeared everyone got the point.

The question didn't need answering.

It could be you.

Another rare moment of silence filled the room.

Bravo, Ms. Williams. Sometimes less was more.

And on to the next chapter—drugs. I forced myself to focus. Ms. Williams' numbers exercise kept intruding on my concentration. Finally, the bell rang. TGIF.

I packed up my book, relieved that we didn't have practice tonight. I could get a head start on homework and start worrying about tomorrow's kind-of-date. I picked up my scrap of paper with number fourteen. I wasn't sure I should have said yes when Matt...

"Hey, Maggie," Matt's friendly voice washed over me. "Number fourteen, huh." He opened his hand to reveal his crumpled paper and smoothed it out on the desk. "Four." He made a tiny ball out of the paper and flicked it toward the trash can. Touchdown.

I crunched my paper in my palm and shoved it in my pocket. "Hi." I smiled, feeling stupid.

"Pick you up tomorrow?" he asked, although it sounded more like a done deal. "8:00?"

I hesitated. Ms. William's numbers exercise, in all of its effectiveness, had scored a hit to my protective armor. He had no way of knowing number fourteen was the *un*-lucky number.

"No, actually, I had a family thing come up..." Crap, the made up excuse spilled from my lips with no actual intention on my part. His smile disappeared; the twinkle in his eye faded. He was disappointed. Really, sincerely disappointed. What was I doing? Rebellion sparked. It was damn well past time I enjoyed life like any normal teenager would.

I could do this.

I could.

"Yeah, so I'll need to meet you there," I finished. I couldn't bring myself to ride in his car, to give him the power to decide when we arrived and when we would leave. I plastered on what I hoped passed for a regretful smile.

Poor Matt, he was surely used to girls being excited about an invitation from him. For the second time, a hint of confusion crossed his brow at my veiled indecision. I half expected him to cancel the invitation. It probably wasn't very nice of me, but all I could think was how cute he appeared with that confused wrinkle on his forehead.

I hoped he didn't mind me driving myself. Suddenly, I really wanted to go.

"Okay, sure," he responded. "I'll see you there."

He wasn't angry or annoyed. Surprised by a bright sense of relief, I smiled for real.

He grinned in return. "8:30?"

I nodded. "Looking forward to it." I heard the ring of truth in my words.

But, less than a minute later, I watched him walk away and wondered again, what had I done?

Chapter Six

I blocked the reality of my abuse for over five years. Until that day Warren walked into the restaurant and blasted through the carefully constructed barriers that contained my nightmares—and my pain.

—Maggie's Journal

I stood in front of the mirror and assessed my jeans, calf-high black boots, and bulky navy blue sweater with a critical eye. My three previous outfits lay strewn across the bed.

After three agonizing days of waiting—and worrying—Saturday night had finally arrived.

Had he asked me out on a *date* or just out with the group? I still wasn't sure—but he *had* offered to pick me up. That was for sure a date. Right?

Now that I was driving myself, however, maybe it was no longer a date. *Aargh!* I knew nothing about dating.

I brushed my hair and pulled it back into a low ponytail. I still wasn't quite sure about the sweater but refused to change again.

Whether it was a date or just a night out with kids from school, it sounded a little scary. And a little fun.

I looked in the mirror one more time.

"Who are you?" the girl in the blue sweater asked.

And despite being nervous—maybe because a girl going on her first maybe-date should be nervous—I smiled.

I'm just a normal girl going on a date.

I glanced at my watch. Almost time to go.

* * *

Thirty minutes later, the bonfire cast long shadows along the lake's shore. Laughter and chatter drifted on the breeze.

I stood at the crest of the hill, gazing down. I'd been standing here in darkness for nearly ten minutes, frozen in place. Smiley normal girl had been shoved aside by scared stiff girl. If this was what normal felt like, maybe I'd been longing for the wrong thing.

What was I doing here?

Shifting my weight from one foot to the other, I stepped from the shadow of a tree into the moonlight—and then debated bolting before anyone saw me.

Too late. Matt spotted me and waved. He separated from the group to head my way. I took a deep breath, then slid down the steep slope to meet him. He welcomed me with a curve of his lips and a twinkle in his eye. He was glad to see me. *Wow.*

"Hey, Maggie. I was starting to worry you wouldn't make it. How was your family thing?"

My family *thing* had consisted of making dinner for my mom, who tended to live on junk food if I didn't cook. "It was good," I responded in a tone that conveyed that topic was now closed. I'd perfected that tone years ago.

What was I doing here? I avoided this type of gathering. This wasn't the first big party I'd been invited to. Just the first one

30

I'd actually attended.

Yep, I'd tamped down my insecurities and discomfort, and sucked it up—and here I was. I'd gotten a little bit excited about a maybe date, about a normal evening—and now I wasn't sure what to do.

I attempted more witty conversation. "Sorry I'm late. Thanks again for inviting me."

"No problem. I'm glad you're here. How about a hot dog?"

"Sounds great."

Placing a hand at the small of my back, he escorted me to the bonfire. My skin tingled where we touched. I wasn't sure if I liked it, and stepped away, trying not to be obvious.

His football buddies approached, greeting me with an array of *heys* and *yos*. We got food, then Matt asked, "Soda or beer?"

Beer. I hid a shudder. "Soda," I answered, a little too quickly, a little too intensely.

Matt quirked an eyebrow and grabbed two sodas. I smiled, relieved that he'd avoided the beer. We found an open spot on a boulder and sat. Enjoying the wood smoked flavor of food cooked over an open fire, I watched the friendly mayhem of kids my age unwinding. Eating, talking, laughing. A few underage drinkers with beers in their hands.

My first party.

"Matt, get off your ass and get more wood," a guy with his arms full of branches called to my kind-of-date.

"Piss off," he yelled back and then turned to me with a grin. "Be right back." He set his plate and drink beside me, a sign he did indeed plan to return.

"Oh my God." Kelvin's strident voice split the pleasant rumble of conversation. With a beer in his hand and face flushed, the D-lineman embodied trouble waiting to happen.

31

"Is anyone besides me tired of hearing about creepos and molyesters?"

His deliberate mispronunciation grated on my nerves, but the crowd laughed.

"Besides, anyone who puts up with that kind of crap needs to grow-a-pair." He drew the words out for emphasis.

Laughter faded into uncomfortable silence. Several kids distanced themselves from an inebriated Kelvin, who snaked an arm around Derron. The wide receiver had the fastest mile in the history of the school, but he'd failed to move quickly enough to escape Kelvin as he continued his rant. "'Specially for a man, you know. Man's gotta stand up for hisself." Keeping an arm around Derron's shoulders, he raised his other fist in the air, then bent at the elbow to show off well-defined biceps.

Derron shrugged out from under Kelvin's arm. "Get off me, asshole."

Kelvin let Derron slip away and snatched a beer from another guy. "Am I right, man, or am I right?" he demanded of Derron, punching him with one fist while swigging beer from the other. "Come on, what self-respecting dude doesn't fight back. Frickin' pussy."

I saw pain flash in Derron's eyes, followed so quickly by rage, I'd have missed it if I hadn't been watching him closely. That pain flashed, and I knew.

Sympathetic anger built inside me as Derron shoved Kelvin back.

"What the hell's your problem? You know I'm right. Ever'body knows Kelvin's right. Man up."

In horror, I watched Derron slide toward loss of control, bunching his fists, eyes flashing. I recognized it—the pent-up anger that threatened to explode and consume everyone in its

32

path. I recognized the biting edge of self-control.

I recognized me.

The crowd grew silent.

"Stop it!" The words spilled out without conscious thought. The unfairness of Kelvin's words spurred me on. "Did you even listen in class? One in four girls and one in six boys. You think all those kids were p—" I couldn't repeat the crude word. "Wimps? You think little kids should man up and punch an adult? You're an ass."

Warmth invaded my face. *Crap.* Certain my cheeks shone bright red, I forced myself to stand my ground. Everyone stared at me, and I wished I could just disappear.

Damn, why couldn't I keep my mouth shut?

I'd probably blown it, drawn unwanted attention to myself, embarrassed Matt in front of his friends, done no one any good.

"Listen here Miss Goody Goody. Ain't nobody gonna diss me that way." Kelvin stalked toward me, his stance threatening.

My heart jumped in my throat. He was a big, big guy.

Then, he stopped. His eyes widened.

"Gotta problem, Kel?"

I turned to see Matt step up beside me. He lifted his arm and laid it across my shoulders.

"She with you?"

"Yeah, she is. And I don't like you disrespecting her." He gave my shoulder a reassuring squeeze.

"Yeah, well, I was just havin' some fun. She a little uptight."

"It didn't sound like fun to me. And can the street talk. Both your parents went to Harvard, and your spoiled ass is headed somewhere ivy league. Put your stupid brains to better use."

Kelvin shrugged. "Sorry," he muttered and walked toward

the shore, guzzling what remained of his beer. I tore my eyes from his retreating form and scanned the crowd. A few people made eye contact and smiled. One boy lifted his glass in silent salute. My eyes clashed with Derron's.

And in that moment we both knew.

Chapter Seven

There's a secret club at every school, and no one knows it exists unless he or she is a member. It defies geographic and socioeconomic boundaries. It welcomes all races, the rich and the poor, the low performing and high achieving. It is perhaps the most inclusive club in the world.

And no one wants to belong.
  —Maggie's Journal

When my gaze locked with Derron's, we shared a fierce and awkward moment of silent communication. I froze, uncertain what to say or do. Because while we might belong to the same crappy club, our club didn't host events. There were no meet and greets. We might recognize each other, but we never *acknowledged* our hated bond.

We were all privately focused on the one club activity—survival.

But still, these moments of recognition lingered, because once you're in the club, you can never get out. And although we didn't openly acknowledge our bond, a strange and disturbing comfort existed in knowing someone understood.

In today's unwilling meeting of members, Derron broke eye

contact first.

Heart still pounding from my unexpected outburst, I jumped when Matt whispered in my ear, "You okay?" I spun and startled again when I found his face mere inches from mine. *Too close.*

Stumbling back a half step I nodded. "Yeah, I'm okay. Listen, I'm sorry, I didn't mean to cause a scene."

He shook his head. "No, Kelvin *was* being an ass. He's a jerk when he drinks too much." Frowning, Matt sought him in the crowd. "If he doesn't watch it, he's going to get himself in trouble one day."

Relieved that he wasn't mad at me for calling out his teammate and anxious to change the subject, I asked, "Want to see if there's any food left?"

"Sure." He searched my face. "He wouldn't have hurt you."

It seemed important to Matt that I believed him. I nodded.

He smiled and held out his hand.

The rawness of the earlier connection with Derron still haunting me, I hesitated. Speculation entered Matt's eyes, but he said nothing, waiting patiently. I bit my lip and placed my hand in his.

It wasn't horrible. And yet my heart picked up pace, unfortunately not in a good way.

I wiggled my toes inside my boots, a mindfulness technique my shrink taught me. It helped me stay in the moment. *This* moment. A good moment.

Toes still wiggling, I concentrated on the feel of my hand in his. It didn't feel exactly good, but it wasn't bad. And one thing I did know—holding hands was normal. I could be normal.

I could. And I would.

We finished our hotdogs and mingled with the crowd, but

the evening's incident refused to leave me alone, even as I grew more used to having Matt's hand clasped with mine. I was finally on a date with a great guy, and I couldn't let go of the past enough to fully enjoy it.

Chapter Eight

Maggie, age 8

When Mommy would not quit crying, Maggie began to fidget. Was she in trouble or not? Was Mommy in trouble? Maggie's lower lip trembled.

Mommy was scaring her.

Then Mommy started talking. "I can't believe...this. Margaret, honey, what exactly...happened?" She took big, gulpy breaths as she talked.

Words stuck in Maggie's throat. *Margaret* was only for getting in trouble. *Honey* was to trick her into thinking she wasn't in trouble.

"Mrs. Bryant," the nice lady from Children's Services offered Mommy a kleenex. "Let's calm down. We talked about this." She gave Maggie's mother the eye, a message Maggie recognized. Ms. Hollis gave kids the eye. The eye meant *don't make me tell you again.*

Then she looked at Maggie. "It's okay. You did the right thing when you told your friend. We're going to figure this all out." She smiled. "While we were waiting for you, we talked about making sure you're in a safe place while we sort this out."

"No!" her mom argued, "You can't take my baby. She belongs

38

with me."

Mommy's shrill voice hurt her ears. Maggie clenched her hands together in her lap. She didn't want to go anywhere!

"Mrs. Bryant, calm down. We already talked about this." The Children's Services lady gave Mom the eye big time, but she smiled at Maggie. "How would you like to stay with your grandma for a few days while we sort this out?

Relief flooded through Maggie. Stay at Grandma's? Grandma made the best cookies. She nodded. "I like staying with Grandma."

Mommy finally stopped crying and gave her a big hug. "Oh, honey, I'll pack your favorite things and bring them over for your fun time at Grandma's."

Maggie smiled. Grandma had a nice room for her. Not a princess room for little beauties.

"You'll be back home soon," Mommy added.

Biting her lip, Maggie thought that maybe, if she was very good, Grandma would let her stay forever.

Maybe she wouldn't have to go back home at all.

* * *

Grandma picked Maggie up from school at the end of the day. When she got to Grandma's house, her clothes and her favorite stuffed kitty had already been unpacked from her purple duffle bag.

"It smells yummy!" Maggie smiled. Her first real smile since the meeting with the lady. "You made cookies." She threw her arms around her grandma and inhaled deeply. Grandma's cookies were the best ever.

She was staying until another nice lady from Children's

Services could talk to her.

Grandma explained that Mommy could visit, but Warren could not.

Maggie flopped down on her bed and clutched Kitty, petting her soft white fur. She buried her nose in Kitty's neck. "Good kitty," she whispered. Her bedroom at Grandma's was nice. It would be perfect if she weren't worried about Mommy.

Grandma helped her with homework, then they had her favorite dinner—spaghetti with real meatballs. That night, Grandma sat on her bed and read her a story about dinosaurs.

Each day Grandma made one of her favorite foods and read one of her favorite stories, and they talked and laughed and had fun.

But they never talked about Warren or the place called Children's Services.

And that was okay, because the only person who opened her door at night was Grandma. She peeked inside while Maggie lay still, hugging Kitty tight, careful not to let Grandma know she was awake.

After a few minutes, Grandma always left, and, finally, Maggie fell asleep.

Chapter Nine

Maggie, age 8

Mommy visited on the Sunday before Maggie's meeting with Children's Services. She brought Maggie's favorite ice cream, Chocolate Chip Cookie Dough, and they sat out back on the old wooden swing that Grandpa built before he died.

It was a sunny day. Maggie's favorite kind. Grandma's flowers waved in the wind. Yellow, red, pink, white, orange. Maggie pretended to stare at the flowers but peeked sideways at her mom.

Eating ice cream with Mommy should have been fun, but instead, it was very, very quiet.

Mommy usually talked a lot. It bothered Maggie that today she didn't say anything.

Tracing the rim of the cone with her tongue, Maggie captured small drips as she cast another glance at her mom. "Are you mad?" she asked in a small voice.

Her mom smiled a big smile with lots of teeth, wrapped an arm around her shoulders, and shook her head. "No, honey, why would I be mad?"

Maggie shrugged. "Because I got Warren in trouble." And because Warren told her every time that her mom would be mad.

Mommy gave her a little squeeze. "Oh, honey, I'm not mad. Look at me. I love you. You know that right?"

Maggie nodded. They continued to swing, licking their ice cream in silence until her mom spoke.

"You were just confused," she assured Maggie. She didn't sound mad.

When Maggie didn't say anything, Mommy squeezed her again. "You know what that means. You thought one thing, but you were wrong. Kind of like an accident."

Maggie knew what confused meant. The only thing confusing her was Mommy. "Mommy, I..."

"Now, honey, you know Warren is an affectionate man. You just misunderstood." She stared into Maggie's eyes. "You exaggerated. Those classes at school, they can make you think things that aren't true. You know you have quite an imagination. Do you understand?"

Maggie's ice cream made her tummy feel sick. She shook her head. She didn't understand.

"On Monday, a lady is going to interview you and you are going to tell her you were wrong. That Warren comes in at night to say good night. That he sometimes rubs your back. That's all. The lady at school, she just confused you. That's all."

"But Mommy, that's not..."

"Oh, baby." She brushed a strand of hair from Maggie's face. "Warren is very angry, but...he's willing to forgive you if you tell the people you made a mistake."

Maggie sat very still. She *was* in trouble.

"If you tell your other story, Warren will be angry." Mommy leaned in close and whispered. "He'll hurt Mommy. You don't want that, do you?" Her voice wobbled.

Chewing her lip, Maggie shook her head.

"And he promises not to go into your room again to say goodnight." Mommy reached up to stroke Maggie's cheek. "Everything will be fine if you do this. Can you do this for Mommy?"

Maggie stared at her ice cream. A line of chocolate chip cookie dough crept down the side of the cone. It fell and landed splat on her pretty shoe. Fighting back tears, she nodded.

Mommy placed her hand on Maggie's knee and squeezed gently. "Honey, I need you to say it. *Warren comes in my room and rubs my back. I exaggerated. I was confused because of what the teacher said.*"

Another slow drop of ice cream wound its way down the cone. "Warren comes in my room and rubs my back. I exaggerated. I was confused 'cause of what the teacher said," Maggie whispered. She was good at memorizing. Mommy knew that.

They swung in silence, ice cream dripping to the ground as Mommy patted her knee in time with the old swing's creaky beat.

And all the while, Maggie stared at the bruise circling her mom's wrist like an ugly bracelet.

* * *

The next week, when the nice lady asked her about Warren, she said exactly what Mommy told her. She'd exaggerated, confused by what her teacher said. The nice lady regarded her with sad eyes and asked if she was sure.

Maggie nodded. "Yes."

She went back home to live with Mommy and Warren. Warren was gone a lot and pretty soon they moved into a different, smaller house, just Mommy and Maggie.

But on those days when he was home, Maggie was nervous all the time. He stopped coming in her room, but she could feel his eyes...

Always watching.

Chapter Ten

Maggie, age 9

In third grade, all the girls wanted to line up with Thomas for square dancing. When he moved, the line of giggling girls moved with him until Ms. Kornfeld finally said, "No more moving. Everyone stay in your line."

On the third day of dancing, the most amazing things happened. He chose the line across from Maggie. On purpose! She was excited. Then nervous. And the excited kind of jitters in her tummy turned into something she didn't understand, and she was scared.

She raised her hand, "Ms. Kornfeld, I don't feel well." Ten minutes later, she was lying down in the health room while Mari danced with her Tommy. The idea of Thomas liking her felt wrong, but she didn't understand why.

The next week, at the meeting where Mommy met with Maggie and her teacher, Ms. Kornfeld said Maggie worked very hard in class, that she studied very hard.

Although Maggie thought this sounded good, the teacher asked if everything was okay at home. She asked it like Maggie had done something wrong.

Mommy made a funny noise before answering, "Everything is fine, isn't it, Maggie?"

Maggie nodded, confused. "I like to study. I can work harder."

Mommy started making that funny noise when her boyfriend, Warren, moved to another city for his job and they moved into the little house.

Ms. Kornfeld smiled, but her smile seemed sad. "Oh, no, Maggie, you work plenty hard." She patted Maggie's hand. "You are a joy to have in class."

Maggie kind of wished she could talk with Mari about it, but they weren't friends anymore. Once, she heard Ms. Kornfeld talking with Ms. Hollis. She said the girls hadn't been close since the *inc'dent*. Maggie wanted to ask what an inc'dent was, but her new friend, Diana called her to come and swing. Diana was nice, but she wasn't a *best* friend.

So, in third grade, Maggie lost her best friend, missed a chance to dance with her secret crush, and became the perfect student.

Chapter Eleven

I've often wondered what my life would be like if I hadn't recanted. Would I be stronger, more open? Would I have more friends? Would I have built this impenetrable fortress around me? The one that keeps out both pain and joy.
    —*Maggie's Journal*

The fight between Kelvin and Derron was quickly forgotten by everyone—everyone except me. After that moment of *knowing* between Derron and me, the excitement of the party dulled. I carefully avoided him. It wasn't difficult. He worked equally hard at staying away from me.

And so while everyone else partied, I pasted on a smile and pledged to put the past where it belonged.

Behind me.

This party...tonight...this was what mattered. I was at a party with a guy who was nice and gorgeous, and, I was pretty sure, interested in me. I glance down at our entwined fingers.

As the night grew later, more and more couples paired off and started to make out. The others became increasingly loud.

When Matt grabbed a beer out of a cooler, the first he'd drunk since I arrived, my palms began to sweat, and my heart began to race. I needed to get the hell out of here.

"Um, I'm sorry, but I need to go," I blurted.

"Huh? Oh, okay. We could go someplace quieter." He waved at the chaotic scene behind him.

"No, really. I need to get home. I have a curfew." The lie flowed easily, joining the one about my family event earlier in the evening. No mom rules governed my behavior. I lived within boundaries I created, and tonight, I had a curfew.

He set the beer back in the cooler. "A curfew, huh?" He chucked my chin. "That's cute."

Relieved that he'd set down the beer, that he wasn't mad because I had to leave, I relaxed. Then his words registered.

Huh. My curfew was cute. Not me. My curfew.

He stepped into my space. Close. Too close. Was he going to kiss me? He *was* going to kiss me. Anticipation built, and butterflies took flight. My heart raced again. This time in a good way.

Then he leaned in, and I panicked, pulling back.

"Well, thanks again for the invitation. I had fun." The words rushed out. The forced smile made an encore appearance. I nodded uncertainly and turned to go.

He touched my arm. I hesitated.

"I had a good time," he said, studying my face.

I fought the urge to squirm.

I swallowed, remembering my earlier outburst. "Yeah, especially the part where I got mad and yelled at your friend." Great. Like he needed to be reminded of that. Whatever. I might shut people out, but when I did speak, I tried to tell the truth. Well, aside from the curfew and the non-existent family thing—and any mention of my abuse.

He laughed. "It was memorable, that's for sure. I'll walk you to your car. To make sure you're safe." We walked a few steps. Then he stopped, his face serious. "Kel was being a jerk. And hardly anyone puts him in his place. You were right to call him on it." He frowned and ran his free hand through his hair. "We okay?"

I nodded.

"You'll probably find this hard to believe, but he can be a really good guy. Maybe after you get to know him, you'll see."

Get to know Kelvin better? *No, I didn't think so.*

We climbed the steep hill in silence. Had it been only a couple of hours ago that I'd arrived, uncertain…scared? I was still scared, but the bad scared battled with excited scared.

Lost in thought, I slipped on a rock, and he grabbed my arm to steady me. His fingers lingered there and then slipped down to grasp my hand. We continued to climb the hill, hand in hand. I was kind of getting used to it. It was…good.

We reached my car all too soon.

Nervousness returned. "Well, thanks again." I withdrew my hand to grab keys from my jacket.

He slipped his fingers in his front pockets, thumbs hanging over the edges. "Want to get a bite to eat sometime? Burgers. Or burritos?"

I searched his face but saw only openness and friendly interest and attraction.

"Uh, sure." Way to sound half hearted. "I'd like that," I added, feeling heat flood my cheeks.

His eyes crinkled. "Okay. How about tomorrow?"

Wow. That was fast.

"Barbecue?" he added, apparently thinking my hesitation

centered around food choice.

I nodded, searching for an answer. Finally, I managed to croak. "Okay."

I was still reeling from the fact that not only had this been a date, but we had another date *tomorrow,* when he leaned in and placed a butterfly kiss on my cheek. It was over so quickly I didn't even realize what was happening until he'd stepped back.

He appeared unaffected by the kiss.

And why would he be? It was just a peck on the cheek. But that soft little kiss had unleashed a horde of wild butterflies in my stomach.

I unlocked the door and sank into the driver's seat. When I tried to shut the door, he grabbed hold of it.

"Drive safe," he said.

Two simple words, but they warmed me. Where the kiss unsettled me, *drive safe* wrapped me in a cocoon of caring.

He shut the door. With a shaky smile, I put the car in reverse. As I drove away, I could see him in the rearview mirror, watching. He stayed there until I turned a corner and drove out of sight.

* * *

That night, I fell asleep to dreams of Matt and holding hands and kisses.

I awoke in the early morning, drenched in sweat, heart pounding. The sweet dreams had twisted and turned until only shades of dark and evil remained. I tried to grasp the memory, but it escaped to be replaced by my mom's voice.

"Wake up, Maggie." She sat next to me, shaking my shoulders.

"Wake up."

I jerked upright, eyes wide. Gulping great gasps of air, I placed one hand placed over my racing heart. "What…what happened?" I rasped.

But I didn't really need to be told, one glimpse of my mom's haunted eyes, and I knew.

After a two year absence, the night terrors were back.

The first night it happened, when I was fourteen, I'd been unable to go back to sleep until I retrieved Kitty, the stuffed white cat I'd carried everywhere in first and second grade. I vaguely remembered putting Kitty on a shelf in third grade, but I'd never quite been able to part with her.

So, at age fourteen, I started sleeping with my kitty again, grasping her to my chest when I woke up terrified at night and tucking her out of sight under the covers in the morning. Like a stupid little kid.

I missed my grandma, who'd died the year before. I missed her cookies and her flowers and the way she helped me feel safe.

I could never remember the nightmares, only the shadows—shapeless and suffocating.

When they failed to lessen after a month, exhausted, I finally told my mom. Color drained from her face, a sure sign something was wrong.

The next week I had my first session with a counselor, Dr. Shirk. She's not really a doctor, but I started calling her Doctor just to annoy her. Even though I actually liked her now, the Doc thing stuck.

It took months of counseling for the full truth of my abuse to emerge. More months to learn how to deal with my new reality and manage my growing anger at my mom.

I'd talked until I was sick of talking. And I realized why Mari and I were no longer friends. Because Mari had confronted me, had cornered me on the playground one day and asked if I was okay. Had tried to talk to me about *it*. But I got angry and told her to go away, that nothing was wrong with me—because I had blocked the abuse.

Poor Mari. Once I realized the truth, I didn't know what to say to make things right. It had been too many years. Or I maybe wasn't brave enough to say what needed to be said.

Maybe I was afraid. Afraid to admit the truth to the girl who had once been my other half. Afraid to confirm what she probably already suspected. That something inside me was broken.

I'd undergone EMDR, Eye Movement Desensitization and Reprocessing, a technique I hated because I had to explore my *feelings* but had to admit helped. Week after week, I held these vibrating egg-shaped things called tappers in my hands while thinking about the things that tormented me. It helped my brain process. Like Drano for the brain.

I'd have preferred to flush Warren down the sewer system where he belonged.

But...thanks to Doc and the weird tappers, I'd made a sort of peace with my past.

All that work and now the damned terrors were back. Doc had warned me about this, that there might be an incident that would trigger their return—news about Warren, stories of others' abuse, but I'd survived those just fine.

Nope, for me, the trigger was apparently an awesome evening with a great guy.

I'd stopped expecting life to be fair a long time ago, but this? Freaking totally and completely unfair. Whatever, I wasn't going in for a *check up.* I'd get through this just fine on my own.

I stayed awake long after Mom left my room, staring at the ceiling, cataloging the creaks and groans of our house. Finally, I threw back the covers and stalked to my closet. Shoving clothes aside, I reached into the back, not caring that several hangars dropped to the floor, leaving my well-kept clothes crumpled in a pile.

Tucked into the farthest corner of the closet, I found her.

Kitty.

Chapter Twelve

*The battle for normalcy wages on several levels. Emotion-
ally, intellectually, physically. It begins each morning
when the alarm clock goes off. It ends...well, in some
ways it never ends. It is the true never-ending story.
Putting one foot in front of the other and living everyday
as though your childhood wasn't ripped from you while
others stood by and let it happen.*
  —Maggie's Journal

I stood in front of my closet for over ten minutes, trying to
decide what a normal girl would wear for a date.

"Everybody your age worries about being normal," the irritating
voice in my head lectured me. I knew that voice. The Doc.

I threw another outfit on the bed, and then slammed the
door shut. *"And besides, normal is so...so booorrriing. You're
just nervous because this is new."* Now my own voice bounced
around in my skull, annoying me further as it picked up where
Doc left off.

"Aargh!" I stomped my foot. I hated it when my rational,
mature self got all preachy and self-aware. Screw it. I was

normal. Everybody had freakin' issues.

And right now, my issue was what to wear on my first real date. Real as in, Matt was picking me up at my house.

Thankfully, Mom wasn't home yet. That would have stressed me out even more. She worked a lot of hours and traveled once or twice a month. She'd failed me in some monumental ways, but I gave her grudging credit for doing her best to provide for us. Although I'm sure she'd have loved to meet Matt, I wasn't ready for that. So, I hadn't told her about tonight.

I stared at the clothes I'd tossed on the bed. This was the second time I'd spent too much time thinking about my clothes because of Matt. Ugh.

I started to worry I was giving him too much power. After all, I'd spent months of therapy taking *back* control of my life. Was I in danger of throwing it all away?

I grabbed the purple sweater and pulled it on. Examining myself in the mirror, I decided I looked nice. Attractive. Not too sexy. I glanced at the other options on the bed. Nope, I wasn't changing again. I liked this sweater, and I refused to allow Matt to overly influence my decisions, no matter how cute and nice he was.

It was normal to worry about what to wear on a date.

Wasn't it?

Now, adding to my stress, I was sick of worrying about worrying. I brushed my hair. Up or down? Ponytail, hairband, or hair flying free in the wind?

I chose the ponytail, then applied blush and mascara.

I took out the ponytail and slipped on the hairband.

I considered the me in the mirror with a critical eye. Maybe I'd go with the hairband for half the date and the ponytail for the other half. I smiled. Amazingly, he hadn't been put off by my unpredictable behavior at the bonfire. I put half my hair in a pigtail, left the other half hanging free. There, maybe he'd like that. I wrinkled my nose and bugged my eyes. Yeah, that was it.

The doorbell rang.

Crap. I pulled the band out of my hair, ran the brush through, put on lip gloss, and headed for the stairs. I shoved the ponytail holder in my pocket. Just in case I needed it.

I paused in front of the door and took a deep breath, then I opened it with what I hoped was a casual air.

"Hey," Matt's eyes twinkled.

I read appreciation in his eyes. It made me nervous.

I kind of wished I'd stuck with the goofy pigtail.

* * *

We enjoyed delicious barbecue, followed by an action movie where we held hands and shared popcorn. He kissed me goodnight, soft and sweet, a lingering, chaste joining of lips that sent tingles all the way to my toes.

As first dates go? Success!

Well, actually, I thought maybe Sunday was our *second* date. After all, we'd held hands and he'd kissed me at the bonfire. I needed a girlfriend to debate this with, and strangely enough, the only friend I wanted to call was Mari. Although we played volleyball together, I hadn't actually had a conversation with her about anything important in almost ten years. So, no call. And since this decision rested solely with me, Sunday officially became our second date—at least in my mind.

On Wednesday, date three, we grabbed a burger and studied. With major tests looming and both of us in advanced classes, the third date received high marks on the date-o-meter. It didn't matter that I had nothing to compare them to. I recognized good—even great—when it landed in front of me.

Another soft kiss at the door. I thought this might be a little *not* normal, but the speed at which we progressed worked for me.

Date four, Saturday, we went out for Chinese with plans to go to another movie afterward. After he told me about Friday's football game and I shared the highlights of my volleyball match, we agreed it was a bummer that our games had conflicted.

Matt's phone buzzed. He glanced at the screen but left it on the table. "Ready for a movie?" His phone buzzed again. He ignored it.

"Uh, do you need to answer that?"

Matt shook his head. "It's just Kel." His phone buzzed a third time.

I raised my brow. "If you need to..." My response faded as he shook his head.

"No, they're just going to the lake again tonight." He smiled. "I have better plans."

"Oh." That was sweet—if he really meant it. Maybe he was just being polite. "But if you want to go..." I let the thought hang there between us. Did he really want to go see a movie with me instead of partying with his friends?

Matt studied my face. "No, I could go if I wanted. But I'd rather be with you. Unless you want to go?"

I bit my lip. I didn't want him to avoid his friends because of me. And it was nice, kind of, that he would take me even though I probably embarrassed him the last time.

"Well, I..." Good grief. I couldn't seem to complete a

57

sentence tonight. Did I want to go? No. But…

Matt placed his hand over mine. "Hey, I know you didn't really like the drinking. And Kel was an ass last time."

Had I been that obvious about the drinking? And Kelvin, well, yeah, he'd been an ass.

"Maggie?"

I realized I'd been quiet for a long time. I inhaled. I really wanted to build a relationship based on honesty. "I don't want you to feel like you can't hang out with your friends. Or have a beer with them." Although I really, really hated beer. "I mean, it's okay, you know."

He remained silent. A frown creased his brow. Then he sighed. "It's kind of obvious you didn't like when I grabbed a beer." He paused and grinned. "And I think you kind of made a face just now when you said *beer*."

I both liked and was worried that he could read me that well. "I don't like the smell of beer. My…" I shut my mouth and stared at my plate. What was there to say? My mom's boyfriend drank? He smelled like beer when he came to my room at night? Hell no, I wasn't saying any of that. I curled my toes in my boots as tension crept up my spine.

Matt squeezed my hand. "Hey."

I looked up into Matt's troubled eyes.

"I don't care if you don't like beer. I don't drink much anyway." He brushed his free hand along his jaw. He looked like I felt. He had something to say but wasn't sure about saying it. Finally, he nodded as if he'd made a decision. "My mom had a brother. He partied a lot in college. Drank too much. Kept drinking after he graduated, although no one really knew he had a problem. He was a functioning alcoholic."

This time I squeezed his hand.

He offered a sad half smile and threaded his fingers through mine. "He died in a car wreck when I was two. DUI. His little girl was with him. Killed her, too." His eyes glistened, and his gaze focused on our clasped hands. "It really messed up my family." He shrugged and looked back at me, his eyes clear. "So I don't drink much, because it would kill my mom if she knew. I don't do things that would hurt my family."

I swallowed. "I'm sorry about your uncle. I didn't know."

"No one around here knows. We don't talk about it."

Okay. I knew all about not talking about it. It made me feel warm inside that he'd told me. And a little guilty that I was keeping my secrets to myself.

Matt stood. "How about that movie?"

I nodded and took his hand. A movie sounded good.

I felt a new closeness between us at the movie, my head resting on his shoulder, sharing popcorn, holding hands. We were good.

But when we left the crowded theatre and wove our way through the other viewers, I saw him. Wyatt Johnson, Warren's nephew. My heart fluttered in panic. Out of the corner of my eye, I saw Matt glance my way and realized I was squeezing his hand.

Aargh! I forced my fingers to relax. Then I wiggled my toes in my shoes as we continued toward Matt's truck, wondering why the hell I was reacting like this. I'd first met Wyatt when Warren dated my mom. He was a year younger than me and went to our high school. Even though Wyatt knew nothing about his creeper uncle's perversions—at least I didn't think he knew—he made me uncomfortable. He was such a Warren Jr., acting like he was God's gift to the world.

Uh, no.

59

I continued to use my mindfulness techniques on the car ride home, but still a sense of doom accompanied us to my front door. Matt, poor guy, remained oblivious. He smiled.

It had been another good date. A great date.

He reached behind my neck and drew me close. *Too close.*

I stiffened.

He hesitated.

"I'm not easy," I blurted. *Easy.* Who even said that anymore? Now, he'd think I was a prude and an idiot. Plus it was our *fourth* date. It's not like I'd never French kissed a guy. I'd kissed a few. Okay...one. Kind of. At a pool party on a rare foray into the social world.

His lips twitched.

"Are you...are you laughing at me?" Heat flushed my cheeks.

"No." A wide smile broke across his face. "The thing is, I've actually never thought you were easy. In fact, you definitely are *not* easy."

I frowned.

He nodded. "I never know what to expect. Half the time I'm not sure you really *want* to go out with me."

"That's not tru—" I stopped as he shook his head, the grin still on his handsome, stupid face. Defeated by his good humor when stating the obvious, I sighed, "It's true. I know. I'm...confusing."

"It's fine. Hell, it's a change. Girls always want to go out with me." His cheeks flushed a little, but I didn't hold his arrogant comment against him. We both knew *that* was true.

"So that's my appeal?" I cocked my head. "That I'm, uh, challenging?"

He wrapped his hands about my shoulders. "Yeah."

Before I could protest, he rubbed his palms from my shoul-

60

ders to my elbows and back. I felt...comforted.

"And you're beautiful."

I tensed. Now I knew he was making stuff up. I wasn't beautiful. Didn't want to be beautiful. *Little beauty.*

"You have pretty blue-gray eyes. They're unique. They sparkle when you laugh." He grinned as if making fun of his own sappiness. "And your hair is gorgeous. And when the sun hits it, it has streaks of red."

Horrified, I felt tears well in my eyes.

"Hey, what?" He looked concerned. "Uh, there's no red. Really."

I placed my fingers over his mouth. "No," I smiled. "Red is fine. My dad had red hair. I never really think I'm like him. So...red is good."

He looked relieved. "So, in addition to being gorgeous, you're smart. And funny when you let loose. Which isn't very often. And you care." He looked embarrassed at these last words. A cocky grin replaced his discomfort. "You don't like me because of football—hell, I think you go out with me in spite of football." He shrugged. "You're brave. Willing to call out BS, like you did w Kel."

I'd been melting at his romantic words. Me—melting! But now? I stiffened. I wasn't brave.

"You're different. Special."

My head started to pound. I wasn't brave, but I *was* different.

What was I thinking? It was only a matter of time until that difference ruined everything.

He leaned forward. My heart pounded. His lips touched mine.

I stepped out of his embrace. Well, it was more like I jerked away as if he had cooties. I tried to recover, even though I

61

knew I'd ruined the moment. "It's getting late. I gotta go in."

"Hey, I didn't mean to offend you." He ran his hand through his hair. "That thing I told you. You know I don't have a drinking problem. It's not like a family thing."

My heart cracked. "I know. I don't think that. Really, it's fine. I...I need to go in." I reached back for the door knob and fumbled to open it.

"Maggie?"

The question in his voice stopped me. We stood on the doorstep, me in the shadows with one foot inside the house, him standing in the full light of the porch.

He ran his hand through his hair. Poor guy, confusion marked his half frown. He stepped back. "I like you. A lot. I thought you liked me."

I stood, frozen, the words crammed together in my throat, unable to break free.

An owl hooted in the old oak on the side of the house. A car drove by with the windows down, the sound of kids laughing and music blaring faded away. Still he waited. He slapped his hand against his thigh.

"Well, I guess that's it then. See you at school." He hesitated again, this poor guy who'd tried so hard to be a good date. Respectful, kind, funny. Honest.

I needed to speak up.

He walked down the sidewalk toward his truck.

I needed to say something...anything to let him know I cared, that I didn't want him to leave.

"I'm sorry," I whispered, quietly, so he wouldn't hear.

He climbed in the cab and slammed the door shut. I watched from the shadowed porch until his tail lights disappeared from sight.

Then I went inside.

* * *

The next morning the unexpected smell of eggs and bacon assailed me as I clomped into the kitchen, tired from tossing and turning all night.

"Good morning, Maggie," Mom greeted me in a suspiciously cheery voice. "I thought I'd surprise you with a good breakfast." She smiled at me as she set food on the table.

Surprise was right. Mom only cooked breakfast on special occasions. And school days never made the cut. On school days it was cereal or oatmeal—and sometimes just a protein bar as I hurried out the door.

Even stranger, the table was set for two people. Usually Mom rushed out the door about the time I entered to grab breakfast. I sat at the table and watched her remove her apron before she joined me, running her hands along the lines of her well-pressed, tailored blue suit.

She tucked her hair behind her ear at least four times during the first two bites, a sure sign she was nervous.

"It's good. Thanks, Mom," I offered. Something was definitely awry.

"I'm glad you like it." Her lips curved, but any attempt at lightness was lost when her lips trembled. She picked at a couple more bites before setting her fork down with a clatter. When she finally spoke, words poured in a rush. "Honey, you've been having night terrors again." Her eyes sought mine. "And last night I heard you crying. I think you should go see Ms. Shirk."

She sat in silence, radiating worry and frustration. She

preferred when I was fine. It made it easier for her to forget her guilt.

Chapter Thirteen

Doc Shirk says we're all broken. If we say we're not, we're lying or denying.

It might be a lie to make me feel better, to feel normal. But then again, the doc doesn't lie that I can tell. Maybe I'm just afraid that if everyone's broken, the world's going straight to hell.
    —Maggie's Journal

Mom was right. I knew she was right. I thought about it off and on all day Sunday, but still, I didn't call on Monday.

I hated when she was right—I'd spent so much of my life certain she was wrong.

One day of not calling and avoiding Matt at school.

Two days.

I avoided him, and yet every time I caught a glimpse of him in the halls, my heart beat a rapid staccato. In the afternoon, he rushed through the door just before the seventh hour bell. I didn't turn away fast enough, and he made eye contact, offering a brief, "Hey."

My words remained stuck, unable to work their way out.

And I still couldn't sleep through the night.

On the third day, I decided to call. I'd like to say it wasn't because of Matt. That I called for me. I guessed maybe I did it for both of us. I liked him, and I'd ruined things between us.

Because of that asshole, Warren.

So, on the fourth day, I gave myself a kick in the butt and called between classes. Damn Doc Shirk. She had a last minute cancellation and fit me in at 2:00.

I had to text my mom so she could call and get me excused from Health Class and volleyball practice. It was all a big pain in the butt. After all, I was almost eighteen. I should be able to check myself out.

As I hustled toward the exit doors after 6th hour, of course, I passed Matt on his way to Health Class.

He nodded, a question in his eyes, no doubt wondering why I was headed in the wrong direction.

I returned the nod and hurried on before he could ask. I pushed the heavy glass doors open and jogged through the blustery fall day to my car. Slamming it into reverse, I zipped out of the parking lot.

I arrived five minutes before my appointment and sat in the parking lot, staring out the windshield. I was never early. Apparently running from Matt topped dreading my shrink session. One minute before the hour, I stalked through the office door. The receptionist shooed me into Doc's office.

"Maggie, it's good to see you." Doc Shirk smiled her welcoming smile. She had warm brown eyes, and despite my complaining, this place comforted me. Like I'd been wrapped in a blanket fresh from the dryer.

But I wasn't fooled. The warmth covered a core of steel. The woman was tough when she needed to be. I shifted in my seat and waited for what I liked to call *the inquisition* to begin. The grandfather clock in the corner tick-tocked, always reliable, like the Doc.

"How have you been?" She put the ball in motion with her standard opening.

"Good."

"I see." She glanced at my legs.

My crossed leg rocked back and forth. Not the casual kind of swing, but the amped up, nervous kind. Crap. Doc just waited. She was a patient woman.

"I'm having night terrors again." I didn't realize until I said it that I felt guilty, like I'd let her down. Not a good feeling for a high achiever.

"That happens."

I liked this about the doc. Nothing shocked her. And she never once has implied that I'm strange. She helped me believe there might be all kinds of normal. Even my kind.

"I went on a date." I blurted. "More than one." There, I'd said it.

"You did?" The warm smile was back. "How was it?"

"Good." I thought about it. "Great, actually." Then, because our sessions are about being honest, I told her about the scene I'd made at the bonfire. How Matt had supported me.

"Do you think you were right to speak up?"

"No...well, yes. I'm not sure. Now, Derron knows that I know." I chewed my bottom lip, remembering the silent acknowledgement that passed between us. "And he knows about me."

She nodded. "How do you feel about that?"

I shrugged. "I guess it's okay."

The grandfather clock ticked in the background.

"Matt doesn't know." I added.

"Do you want him to know?"

"No." I responded too fast.

"Okay." She waited. The woman was patient. I both liked and hated it.

"Maybe. Besides, we broke up. Well, I guess we didn't actually break up because we only went out a few times. I'm uncomfortable when we get close. You know…" I raised my eyes to hers.

Again, she nodded.

"At first, I feel good, but then I get scared."

"Why are you scared?"

I said nothing.

"Are you afraid of him?"

"What? No…not like that."

Tick…tock…tick…tock.

"What if he knows?" I finally asked.

"What if he does?"

I liked that she didn't ask *knows what*. I didn't answer. For a long time.

"What if he does?" she persisted.

I couldn't say it.

"Maggie, what if he does?"

"He'll know it's my fault!" I regretted the words as soon as they left my dumb mouth. I knew it wasn't my fault, but knowing and *knowing* weren't the same.

I started to cry. Dammit!

She handed me a tissue.

"What's your fault, Maggie?"

"Nothing. Except that *he* still has the power to influence my

68

decisions and my feelings." I parroted the words from sessions past. But I meant them. And we both knew I was no longer talking about Matt.

"That's right. Nothing was your fault. *Nothing.*"

"What if I tell Matt and he doesn't like me? What if he...judges me?"

Before she answered, I already knew what she'd say.

"What if he doesn't like you? What if he judges?"

I didn't want to say it. He was a girl's dream. Cute and sweet. Strong and smart. Pretty much perfect.

"Maggie? What if it makes a difference? What if he judges?" She pushed me to say it.

"Then he's not good enough for me." I gritted out the words and almost believed it.

"Damn straight." She nodded approval.

I smiled for the first time since I'd arrived. Then, another fear intruded.

"What if..." The unwelcome thought trailed off. I knew what she'd say, but the truth was the truth. Right?

"What if..." She peered over her steepled fingers.

"What if he realizes he's...*too* good for me?"

Doc Shirk sighed. "Maggie, different side of the same coin." She leaned forward, her face all earnest. "Secrets keep us sick. If you can't be honest and authentic in a relationship then it's not real. It's not worth it."

She let me sit in silence while I mulled this over.

She was right. Of course, she was right. I nodded. "Okay."

And yet...it might be worth it for a little while. Even as the thought flitted through mind, I knew it was wrong.

And yet...

Chapter Fourteen

Peck, peck, pecking. Pecking away at my brain like a woodpecker eating the nasty bugs.
  —Maggie's Journal

"Do you think it would be helpful if we did EMDR?" Doc called me back from my internal debate over the short- and long-term benefits of honesty.

No. "Yes," I spoke reluctantly. I didn't like EMDR, Eye Movement Desensitization and Reprocessing, but it had helped with the nightmares last time. "Let's do it," I added with more conviction.

I scrunched further down in the padded leather chair. I scooted a little to the right, then to the left, then crossed and uncrossed my legs. Nope.

I tucked my left foot under my right knee. Ah, okay, that was comfy. I could do this. Be all calm and cool and talk about my *feelings*. Ugh.

Doc Shirk smiled. "Better?"

I rolled my neck to the right and then the left. It popped once. "Better."

It's silly, I know, but I had to be just right physically to dig into my emotions.

"So, Maggie, what's bothering you the most?"

"I'm angry." With those two words, my laid back self slunk into hiding. "Angry that there's this nice guy and he likes me and I like him." I paused. Sharing really wasn't my thing. I wiggled my toes. "I was kind of daydreaming about...us and kissing and stuff when I fell asleep a few nights ago. Then I started dreaming about...well, I don't really remember except it was dark and scary and horrible! Then I woke up all sweaty, and my heart was pounding. And I'm pissed." Both feet hit the floor and started tapping.

"If you don't remember, what are you mad about?" The friendly curiosity in her voice annoyed me even further.

"I know it's because of Warren even if I don't remember, and I don't want him having freakin' control over me." My voice sounded overloud to my ears. So much for being cool.

"Okay, what bothers you the most when you think about Warren?" Her calm voice settled over my agitated one.

I tried to pick only one thing. "I hate the way he smells. He wears some spicy aftershave." I thought some more. "Mostly I hate his voice. The way he called me 'little beauty.' Asshole." I inhaled deeply through my nose and exhaled through my mouth. My feet quit tapping.

"When you think about his voice, what negative self-talk do you have?"

We'd discussed this before. "I'm in danger..." My voice trailed off.

"You're in danger...?" The question hung in the air.

I nodded. "I'm in danger, and it's my fault." I hate-hate-hated this. "He does *it* because of me. I feel...guilty...worthless."

71

"Okay." Her voice remained calm, and I needed that. "What would you like to think about yourself in this situation?"

The answer came easily. We'd been through all of this when I was fourteen. And fifteen. So, I'd had a year-and-a-half of being reasonably well-adjusted—and thinking that maybe, someday, I could be normal.

"That it's over. I'm safe. He's out of my life." I stuck my left foot back under my right knee. "That I didn't do anything to deserve what happened. He's the one who's guilty. *He's worthless.*" I stared right at her. "I'm a good person."

"Let's think about the danger first. How true do you think your positive thought is—that you're safe—on a scale of one to seven? One is totally false and seven is true."

"A two." And I wanted to bang my head against the wall. *A two!* I used to be at least a five or six.

I knew I wasn't in danger, that I wasn't at fault. That I had value. But that's not how I *felt*. Right now, I didn't *feel* like the abuse was over, like Warren was out of my life.

"Maggie," Doc called for my attention. "How do you feel when you think about Warren and the words 'I'm in danger' and 'It's my fault'?"

How do I feel? "I feel scared and worried...and pissed! Why did this happen to me? It's so unfair."

"Okay," she continued, her voice soothing. "How disturbing is this thought on a scale from zero to ten?"

"A nine," I blurted, and it surprised me. A nine after all this time.

"Where do you feel it in your body?"

I'd always thought it strange, but the doc taught me that our bodies held memories. "I feel it in my stomach." The same place as always. Sometimes in my head, but always in my gut.

"Now we'll begin processing. I'm going to turn on the tappers for about thirty seconds and then stop. During this time you just let your mind go where it wants to. Or daydream. You can close your eyes or keep them open if that's more comfortable. Just let whatever happens happen."

She handed me little egg-shaped flat things that vibrated in my hands. I thought it stupid they were called tappers. They don't tap! Sometimes I call them zippy zappers, but never out loud. I...

"Maggie?"

I sighed, settled back into the chair and closed my eyes, one *zapper* clutched in each palm.

"When I think you've processed your thoughts, I'll turn off the tappers," she reminded me. "After we stop, I'll have you take a deep breath and refocus. I will ask you to just report what you're noticing without thinking about whether it makes sense or not."

Silence settled in the room.

"Focus on the thing that bothers you the most."

The tapper in my right hand vibrated.

"How's my little beauty."

The left vibrated.

I hated his voice, those words.

The right vibrated.

My head filled with such fury, I didn't understand how my brain didn't just explode.

The left vibrated.

"Afraid of the dark? It's okay, Uncle Warren will stay with you until you fall asleep."

The right vibrated.

"There's no need for a night light, Tina."

73

The left.

"I'll stay with her." He held my hand, his big fingers entwined with my tiny ones.

The right.

Isn't that better, little beauty?"

The left.

"Yes."

The right.

"Let me rub your back."

The left.

"Doesn't that feel good, little beauty?"

The right.

"Yes."

The left. The rhythm tempted my racing thoughts, calling them to ride the current, until the vibrations faded into the background and I had only the horror of my memories.

"I brought us each a piece of your favorite candy."

"But, Mommy..."

"It'll be our secret, little beauty. We won't tell Mommy."

"Okay."

"Let's cuddle. There's no need to worry, little beauty. Doesn't this feel nice."

"Yes."

"Yes, Uncle Warren," he insisted.

"Yes, Uncle Warren."

"Do you like this?"

No. *"Yes, Uncle Warren."*

Candy, sparkly and pink, rained down on the bed.

"If you ever tell your mom, you'll have to leave."

"You won't have a home." Light flashed in the room. Warren smiled as he said the words, his teeth huge in the blinding brightness.

"It will kill your mom." Darkness snuffed out the light, leaving the room in layers of black so dark, no shadows remained.

"You won't have this nice room, you won't have anywhere to live."

The last piece of candy dropped to the floor. It rolled and rolled and rolled and...

It wouldn't stop.

"Don't make me hurt your mom."

"Does this feel good, little beauty?"

"Yes."

No!

"No!"

The right vibrated.

The left.

No.

I inhaled a deep cleansing breath.

The vibrations ceased.

Tick-tock. Tick-tock. The clock picked up the rhythm, relaxing me. I took a deep breath.

"What did you notice?" She asked softly.

"Darkness, his voice, falling candy. Saying yes but wanting to say no. Bright light. Darkness." I shrugged. I didn't like to talk a lot afterward. Some people talk a lot, others don't. Either is okay according to Doc. I opened my eyes.

She smiled at me. "Shall we do it again?"

I nodded and clutched the zappers tight.

* * *

We repeated the process two more times. After each zippy zap experience, I shared my memories and crazy visions with Doc.

After the last time, I handed the weird little things back.

Doc Shirk set them aside, watching me intently. "On a scale of one to ten, how much does the memory of Warren bother you now?"

"A five, maybe a six." A calm had settled into the spinning recesses of my mind, leaving a five in place of the stupid nine. "A five," I repeated, feeling strangely optimistic.

"I think it might be good for you to return in another week or two."

"Okay." I'd be dreading the plunge into memories and weird visions by the time the next session arrived, but right now I couldn't argue with results. Zippy zap was weird, but it worked.

Doc explained in one of our early sessions that the brain stores traumatic memories in the primitive part of the brain, the fight or flight area. The brain doesn't know what it needs, so it takes in everything and stores it all. Once I stopped blocking the memories, everything flooded back—all kinds of crap I didn't need or want. Crap that sometimes haunted me in nightmares.

In night terrors.

Crap that had messed up my relationship with Matt.

"Remember, your brain will keep working on this after you leave. Use your imaginary container to put it away until you come back." Doc pulled me back to the present.

I nodded, picturing my graffiti-covered trash can—make believe and yet very real. My mind would stuff Warren in that trash can, and I'd padlock it shut. Then I'd mentally wrap the whole thing in duct tape. I kept the crap safely locked away until my next session.

Doc offered to let me leave the can in her office, but I carried it with me...just in case.

One day, I was going to stop lugging the can back to her office. One day, I'd take that damn can of Warren trash and weight it down with cement blocks and dump it in the Missouri River. One day, the padlock would rust off and the little fishies would have a feast.

One day.

But today, I'd focus on a smaller step forward.

I felt better, stronger...it was time to tell Matt the truth. And he had shared his family secrets with me. I could confide in him.

He was worth it...and so was I.

Chapter Fifteen

I think I'm an optimist by nature, but life has tried to paint me otherwise. Sometimes, I have little glimpses of me as a young girl. Before Warren. Every day was full of possibilities. I'd meet a prince. I'd slay a dragon. I'd fall in love.

Girls who haven't been abused are so innocent.
  —Maggie's Journal

I thought about texting, "Can we talk?" I even typed it in, but hit cancel at the last minute. Texting was the coward's way out. If I wasn't brave enough to ask Matt in person, I thought maybe I didn't deserve a second chance.

I'd figured this out myself. I didn't even need Doc to point me in the say-it-to-his-face direction. Matt thought I was brave. I took a deep breath. I wanted to live up to his opinion.

Be brave.

I spent Tuesday night getting my courage up, which was good because I ran into Matt first thing Wednesday morning. I turned a corner and—there he was.

"Hey, you okay?" Sincere concern sounded in his voice.

"Yes, why?" I fought the urge to check my hair and clothes. Did I *look* like something was wrong?

"You missed class yesterday." He shrugged. "You never miss."

"Oh, yeah, I had an appointment." I set my shoulders and prepared to...

"Mags had an appointment." Kelvin's voice sounded close to my ear, interrupting me. His breath blew across my skin, causing me to jerk sideways.

I started to come around with a right hook but stopped myself before I made another scene in front of Matt's friends.

"Back off." Matt frowned. Thank God, the frown was directed at Kelvin and not me.

"Hey, I was just kidding around. She's prickly." Kelvin glared at me.

"Uh huh. Your breath probably stinks. She had to get away," Matt countered.

I calmed as Matt drew attention away from my overreaction.

"Snappy comeback, bro." Kelvin smacked him on the arm. He smiled at me. "Later, Mags."

I hated that stupid nickname.

We watched Kelvin walk away until Matt broke the silence. "Well, I'd better go."

I nodded, and we went in opposite directions, my opportunity to talk with him lost.

I didn't talk to him again Wednesday.

I did speak with him Thursday, but nothing more than a chat about class. But still, I'd made progress.

Friday arrived, and I was finally ready. At least that's what I told myself during breakfast, over lunch, during passing time between classes, and at least a dozen times when I should have been focusing on a teacher's lecture. When the bell finally rang after health class, I was exhausted.

And scared.

Everyone hustled out the door, the freedom of Friday smiling on their faces. I trudged after, my own smile forced. A smile poor Matt was all too familiar with.

I took a deep breath, still smiling, and I stepped out the classroom door. Matt lounged in the hallway, talking with Kelvin. Great. The friend I least liked—and I was pretty sure good buddy Kelvin returned my feelings with an extra dose of disdain.

I'm brave. I have the power. I repeated the words in my head as I forced myself forward.

"Hey, Matt," I called as I neared.

His head jerked around. His eyes met mine. I'd shocked him. After a week of mumbling a quiet *hi*, and offering nothing more unless he started the conversation, I had spoken first. Heck, I'd actually called out to get his attention.

He said something to Kelvin, who rolled his eyes before walking away.

Matt stepped toward me. The passing students faded away as we stared at each other. He waited...as he had before. I understood. It was my turn.

"Hi." I winced at how lame it sounded. "I was wondering if we...could we talk? Maybe grab a hamburger tonight after the game. My treat."

He frowned and peered past me. Not the response I was hoping for.

"Matt!" Brandi called from behind me. She slipped between us and linked her arm through his. "Still coming tonight?"

She batted her eyes. Honest to God, batted her heavily

80

mascaraed eye lashes. She cornered the market on flirting, sporting a low-cut, tight-fitting white sweater and a skirt so short I don't know how it passed dress code. I prayed the floor would open up and swallow me. He already had plans. And from the evidence, those plans included Brandi.

He smiled. "Thanks for the invite, but I won't be able to make it tonight."

What? He was turning her down? My heart raced.

Brandi pouted prettily. "We'll miss you. Sure I can't change your mind?"

He shook his head. "I have plans."

Oh. He had plans. Well, sure, a guy like him would already have plans. What was I thinking?

Brandi cast a curious glance my way.

I bit the inside of my lip. She clearly thought his plans included me. *Me?*

"Okay." She squeezed his arm, pulling it tight against her chest. "Maybe another time." She spun around and headed down the hall, calling, "Hey, guys, wait up!"

"Maggie?"

Oh crap. I snapped my mouth shut, aware too late that it was hanging open.

I slapped the smile back on my face.

Matt stared at me. The corner of his mouth turned up just a bit. "Pick you up after the game?"

"Yeah." Matt had plans—with me. I relaxed a little. My smile eased into something natural. Matt must have noticed, because his eyes crinkled at the corners. "See you then."

As I hustled down the hall to volleyball practice, my relief morphed into nerves.

Did I have to tell him the truth? Or could I just be less weird, and everything would be okay?

Because if I was going to talk to someone about what had happened—someone who wasn't Mom or Dr. Shirk—it would be the first time I'd told the truth since I recanted.

* * *

I raced home after practice, showered, and was ready by 6:30. I wore a dark purple fleece pullover and jeans. Light makeup. My favorite boots. Comfort clothes. I didn't change my outfit even once.

I'd like to say it's because I was so full of self-confidence, but really, I was too busy deciding whether to tell him the truth about my past or whether to just quit running hot and cold with him. Uh huh. Like it would be easier now than it was on our first dates.

The thing is, I wasn't sure I could be *normal* enough without being honest about my past. But did telling the truth guarantee I'd be *not normal* forever?

Aarrgh!

So the truth was that I was so nervous about how and when and what to tell Matt about my past that I didn't have any room left for worrying about something as unimportant as clothes.

"I'm going to the game," I called over my shoulder as I hustled out the door. I figured being nervous at the game was better than going crazy at home waiting for Matt.

When I arrived at the game, I almost chickened out. The crowd was overwhelming, but I'd never watched Matt play, and tonight, I wanted to do everything right.

He was amazing. Big, strong, quick. His guy never made it past him. I could see why colleges were courting him. Our team was favored to go all the way to the state championship, and Matt was a big part of their success.

My guy.

At least I hoped so.

After the game, I waited with the other students for the team to exit the field. They clomped along the asphalt, cleats noisy, uniforms dirty, players sweaty and smiling. When Matt passed by, he seemed to catch a glimpse of me out of the corner of his eye. His head jerked in my direction, as if startled by my presence.

He cut through the players to stop in front of me. "Hey," he offered, beaming with pleasure—and more than a little surprise.

Who could blame him after the way I'd behaved?

"Good game." Me with the snappy repartee.

"Yeah, thanks." He smiled. "Pick you up in thirty minutes?"

"See you then." I replied.

He turned and jogged after the team. My heart thudded, a combination of both excitement and dread.

* * *

The doorbell rang at 9:30. I let Mom get the door. I never did that. I didn't really like her talking to the occasional friend I invited to my home.

"Well, hello." Mom's cheery voice floated down the hall. "You must be Matt."

"It's nice to meet you, Mrs. Bryant," Matt responded.

I couldn't help but smirk despite my stress. He used his super respectful voice, the one usually reserved for the football coach. Mom probably thought I'd really brought home a prize.

And she'd be right. He was a good guy.

I headed down the hall. *He's a good guy*, played over and over in my mind.

"Hi." I nodded. A tingle of excitement ran up my spine. He was gorgeous in a dark blue v-neck pullover and jeans. A lock of dark brown hair fell on his forehead, and I wanted to brush it back. Not because it was out of place, but just to touch it. To touch him. The desire to connect with him physically, to brush his hair, hold his hand, surprised me.

I realized he was staring at me. Watching me watching him.

"Don't be out too late." Mom broke the spell in that extra-chipper voice.

"Don't worry, Mrs. Bryant. I'll have her back in time for her curfew."

Damn.

Mom laughed. "Curfew? Aren't you sweet."

We hustled out the door as fast as we could.

Matt opened my door, and I slid into his truck, avoiding eye contact. He hopped in and started the car. We just sat there. Finally, he sighed, "No curfew, right?"

I glanced his way. "No curfew."

We stared at each other. I could see his disappointment that I'd lied.

"You have a thing for girls with curfews?" I snapped. Completely unfair, I knew even as the words spewed out.

He ran his hand through his hair. "What's the deal? *You* invited *me* out. Don't…don't act like I'm a jerk."

He appeared embarrassed by his protest, but I understood his point. He was right.

"You either want to go out with me or you don't." He waited, fingers tapping against the steering wheel. That special

84

moment after the game gone in a poof of my stupidity.

Color drained from my face. We weren't even five minutes into the date, and I was making a mess out of everything.

"I do. Want to go out. And I'm sorry." I bit my bottom lip. "How about I buy you dinner and then explain?" I offered a small smile. Inside, my heart pounded. It looked like I was going to tell him something about my past.

"Sounds good." He nodded.

We drove in not quite comfortable silence. Then he reached over and took my hand. We laced our fingers together and everything was okay.

For now.

Chapter Sixteen

The other people, the ones who weren't abused, who aren't damaged—sometimes I can't help but wonder...are they worth more than me?
—Maggie's Journal

Dinner went well. We talked about school and sports—safe subjects. Friends, mostly his, from school dropped by our table from time to time as we munched our hamburgers.

After dinner, we went to the lake. At first, we just walked. A breeze blew. It wasn't cold really, but still my hand shivered in his. It was time for the truth.

We stopped under the spread of an old maple, its leaves ripping one-by-one from the branches and twirling through the air. The full moon reflected so brightly on the lake that I could watch their brilliant color determinedly carpet the brown earth.

I glanced out at the lake, thinking about the geese, the incoming storm, our first kiss. About where things were headed...and if I was ready for more.

It wasn't just the increasing physical contact. It wasn't even telling him the truth about my past. It was revealing my emotions, revealing *me*, that scared me most.

"Hey," he called softly.

I turned reluctantly.

Worried brown eyes stared back. "Are you okay?"

I nodded and laughed self consciously. "Not really...maybe." I'd lied enough, little white lies, but still...lies. "I'm, uh, a little nervous about what I have to say."

He stepped close and took both of my hands in his, squeezing reassuringly. "You can talk to me." He sighed. "Maybe that sounds, I don't know, like I'm full of myself. I just, well, there's something about you. I hope you feel like you can trust me."

The wind blew red leaves in a small whirlpool at our feet. A strand of hair broke free from my ponytail. Matt captured it and tucked it back behind my ear. I did trust him. Sure, he'd treated me well and that was important. But also, there was something between us. Like, we clicked.

I took a deep breath and plunged in. "Do you remember that day in Ms. William's class?"

His brow wrinkled in confusion.

Stupid question. He needed to know which day. "The day we talked about predators." Maybe that would be enough.

He smiled. "The day I asked you out."

Frowning, I tried again. "No. I mean yes, that day. And then that weekend at the bonfire when Kelvin was being an ass, and I, well, kind of lost it."

His smile faded.

"The thing is..." Ah damn. Why couldn't I just say it? Because I was afraid it would ruin everything, that he would find out how not normal I really was. "The thing is, those statistics..." I couldn't say it.

87

He searched my face. I watched him closely and saw only curiosity and kindness followed by the light of understanding.

"You know someone." He nodded. "That's why you got mad at Kelvin. You didn't lose it. You were brave. The only one willing to say what we all were thinking." He tucked the lock of hair behind my ear again, apparently unaware his efforts were useless in this wind.

I fought the urge to stomp my foot. Why didn't he get it? *Why couldn't I say it?* Because except for the sessions with Dr. Shirk, the last time I'd told the truth had been in second grade. And I knew how well that had worked out.

"The thing is, I don't just *know* someone." My heart beat hard.

His eyes widened, the kindness replaced by confusion and then slowly dawning horror. He was beginning to really understand.

"I...I am someone. I was abused." *Ohmygod, ohmygod.* The cat was out of the bag. I thought of Kitty, hidden deep inside my closet. I sucked in another breath and forced myself to calm down.

I wished that perhaps the moon wasn't so bright, that the distant clouds would hurry and overtake the moon, that the water rocked with turbulent waves instead of resting smooth as glass in the gentle breeze. Because the moon's reflection revealed how the color drained from his face. It allowed me to read the questions in his troubled eyes.

"When I was eight, my mom's..." I hesitated. If I provided too many specifics, he could figure it out. Social media lived forever. "A friend of my mom's abused me."

His jaw tightened. The tiny tic I'd seen before jumped along his jaw.

Suddenly, I worried I was wrong to have told him. Not because he'd judge me, but because it wasn't fair to place this burden on him. The burden of truth.

"You were abused."

Not a question, but still I nodded.

"Sexually."

Again, not a question. Again, I nodded.

"When you were just eight years old." His face turned an odd shade of green in the moonlight, like he was going to throw up. "Were you, did he...?"

"He never raped me." I barely recognized my own voice, it sounded harsh, hoarse. I'm sure he had to strain to hear. Warren had never raped me, but that didn't lessen the horror or confusion or guilt of a little eight-year-old girl. Didn't limit the damage to a young woman.

On the verge of disappearing into the nightmare of my past, I wiggled my toes in my boots, grounding myself here, in the present. "He touched me. He was careful not to do anything that would...leave evidence."

I'd said it. Relief flooded through me. I'd said it.

He trembled just before he let go of my hands and walked away.

Chapter Seventeen

Although I know it's stupid and wrong, this question gnaws at my gut—if people find out will they think it was my fault?
  —Maggie's Journal

Kicking at the ground, he stalked to the lake's edge. Dirt and twigs flew in his wake. Leaves leapt and whirled, caught by the wind each time he disturbed them. He halted on the shore and stared out. The breeze whipped his hair. Had the wind become more intense, or were my rioting emotions impacting my view of the night?

His fist clenched and unclenched at his side. A cloud passed in front of the moon, shrouding us in gray.

I didn't know what to say. I worried that I'd already said too much.

Minutes passed, and my earlier feelings of relief faded under the rapid beat of my heart. My fight or flight response kicked in, and I fought the urge to flee.

Then, it occurred to me. It had taken me years to come to terms with the truth. I owed him more than a couple of minutes.

Another minute passed. And another. And another. When the wind picked up again, it chased the clouds from overhead, and the full moon again shone so bright it bathed him in light from both the sky and the water's reflection. The longer I waited, the calmer I became. I didn't really understand it—or maybe I did. I was more worried about him than about me.

The realization was weirdly freeing.

I walked toward the shore and stopped a few feet away. I needed to be close, needed to know, and yet I couldn't bring myself to study his face.

Although I said nothing, he must have heard me approach. He spun and stumbled on his first step, as if unable to fully control his actions, then covered the remaining space between us in two long strides.

His face blurred before my eyes. I raised a trembling hand to my cheek, swiping the dampness from my skin. He wiped the remaining tears gently with his fingertips before pulling me into a tight embrace. It was fierce and hard. This time his touch didn't comfort me, but it didn't scare me either.

Not until I realized that maybe he was saying goodbye.

"I'm sorry," he whispered. Not that husky voice I loved, but a harsh protest, torn from deep inside his chest. His lips moved against my hair. "I'm sorry."

Abruptly, he released me.

I stared at the ground. It was over. *We* were over. When I'd only just begun to understand what being a *we* meant. My heart stopped racing. It just...stopped.

I dug my toe into the dirt, not caring that I scuffed my favorite boots. I'd never be able to wear them again without thinking about this difficult, confusing, soon-to-be miserable night. "It's okay. It's a lot to take in. Please don't feel bad. I just wanted you to know. It wasn't you. You were great. Really." I needed to stop rambling. "You should take me home now."

I still hadn't been able to look at him. When he didn't respond, I peeked at his face and found it set in hard lines. The tic pulsed along the tense lines of his jaw.

He was angry.

Angry!

He scraped one hand through his hair. "I said I'm sorry because I'm sorry this happened to you when you were a little girl. I'm sorry I wasn't there to beat the crap out of the guy."

I stared, shocked by his response.

"What did you think I meant?"

I wanted to back peddle, but I'd promised myself that tonight I'd be honest. "I uh, thought you were breaking up with me." Great. This honesty stuff kind of sucked. "Not that we're an item or anything."

"Shut up," he rasped. Normally that would tick me off, but it sounded more like a caress than an insult. "Don't be stupid."

My eyes narrowed. It was one thing for me to feel stupid, but another for him to say it. My anger faded with his next words.

"I like you. This…it doesn't make me like you less. It makes me angry."

He took my hand and entwined our fingers. "I need time, but I don't need time away from you." He gently tugged, and we started walking.

Hand-in-hand, we rambled along the shore. I could practically hear the thoughts churning in his mind. I curled my fingers into his. I was getting good at this hand-holding thing.

"Is he in jail now?"

I hesitated, unsure how much to tell him. Honesty didn't require full disclosure. Did it?

"Maggie?" he prodded. The edge of anger rang again in his voice.

Although I knew he wasn't angry with me, I still dreaded this conversation. "He's not in jail."

His grip tightened, and tension flowed from his body into mine.

"When did he get out?"

I wanted his conversation to end and yet each word wrenched slowly, painfully from my throat. "He...never went to jail."

"You never told anyone?" He sounded indignant. He squeezed my hand again, a sign of support. "I mean, it's okay, I just...I want the bastard to suffer."

I remained silent.

"Did you ever tell?"

I was going to have to tell him everything. Biting my lip, I realized I hadn't thought this part through. "I did. But later I recanted. I said I'd made a mistake." Better to get it all out at once. My heart pounded in my ears.

"You rec...why?" He stopped walking and searched my face. "Why?" His voice dropped, more demand than question. He needed an answer.

The words stuck in my throat. It was one thing to reveal the abuse, but to confess the next part...that my mom valued me so little...

I whispered, "Because my mom told me to say I'd made a mistake."

At his sharp intake of breath, I swallowed hard.

"That's not right. Why would she do that?" He stood frozen

93

in place before me, confusion and disbelief etching lines in his brow.

"I don't know." Nervous energy sent me pacing along the shore, and his hand latched onto mine, he followed. We stalked the shore until I gathered the words, fundamental and true—and woefully insufficient. "She was afraid."

Mom and I had talked about this exactly once since the night terrors brought everything crashing back. How was I supposed to make him understand when I never had?

"Of what?"

The million-dollar question. I shrugged. "Of him." Maybe a little of what people would think. Although she'd never told me this, deep inside, I'd always wondered if it was true.

The tic returned. "What happened? Did he keep—"

"No, after I told, he never touched me again. They quit…being friends a couple of months later."

I could tell he was wondering what kind of mom ignored something like this, continued a relationship of any kind for months. I had no answer for him.

"And you never told anyone else?"

I shook my head, then added, "Well, I see a counselor sometimes." I felt even more exposed, admitting this. *I saw a shrink.* "She's nice," I added irrelevantly.

He frowned. "Doesn't she have to tell somebody?"

Relieved the shrink thing didn't bother him, I grew concerned about his stubbornness. He was a dog with a bone about reporting. Sure, in his world people received justice. My world didn't make sense to him. I squeezed his hand. "Yes, she would have reported."

"But nothing happened?"

"No. I'd already recanted."

"Because your mom convinced you to." This time it wasn't a question. The truth was sinking in. "She *made* you recant."

I nodded.

"That's not right." He smacked his palm against his leg. Once, twice, three times. "What the hell's wrong with her?"

"She was afraid of him." I repeated my earlier response. Really, what else was there to say?

"Afraid?"

My explanation hadn't fully penetrated the bubble of what's fair and right that surrounded him.

"Yeah, afraid he'd hurt her. Afraid he'd hurt me. And he had...connections. Powerful connections. Anyway, he moved away." The words rushed out. The true story of my youth, slightly abridged.

He dropped my hand and stumbled backward, anger radiating in every movement, and I was afraid. Not afraid of Matt, but of what he might do. He wanted to protect me, but he didn't understand. I was the one who had to protect him. I could never tell him Warren's name.

"This is bullshit," he muttered to himself, but I heard each word. He stared at me. "It's not right."

It wasn't right. And it wasn't fair. And worse, I had brought this darkness to Matt's doorstep. Sure, he knew life wasn't fair. He'd lost his uncle and cousin. But he'd been little at the time and hadn't experienced the full punch to the gut. He'd been living his nice life, being a nice guy. I wished I hadn't been the one to destroy his mostly bright and shiny view of the world.

Chapter Eighteen

Life isn't fair.
   —Maggie's Journal

Color flooded back into Matt's face. His mouth opened and closed and opened again. Nothing came out. I think he was trying to prevent his frustration from spewing out and suffocating me.

Silence grew between us. Poignant at first, and then just plain awkward.

Too awkward for me.

I pulled my hand from his. As my fingers slid from his grasp, his hands clenched. He captured the tips of my fingers and tugged me straight into his arms. Wrapping me close, he rested his face alongside my hair.

"I'm sorry this happened to you," he whispered again, his embrace less fierce this time, more comforting.

His body trembled. I wrapped my arms around his strong shoulders and patted his back, humbled by his response. "It's okay," I whispered. "It was a long time ago. It's okay."

He pulled back abruptly, his eyes glistening in the moonlight.

Tension raced through his body until he was strung so tight he shook from the self-control required to contain his emotions. When he spoke, he bit out each word in a too-calm voice. "Who is he?"

My eyes narrowed. "Why do you want to know?"

"Because I'm going to beat the crap out of the pervert."

It took a second for the words to register. He'd spoken in the tone he might use if he'd said, "I'm going to invite him to lunch." *Hell no.*

"I'm not going to tell you who he is. I don't need anyone fighting my battles."

I could tell he wanted to argue. But I also saw that he was already treating me differently, weighing his words carefully, like I was fragile. I punched his arm. Hard.

"What the hell?" He startled and rubbed the spot where I hit him.

Uh huh, I'm pretty sure my hand hurt more than his arm. The guy was all muscle.

Thankful that I'd broken through his false calm, I clarified my position. "I'm not fragile. I don't need to be protected. I just wanted you to understand. It wasn't you."

He shoved his hands in his pockets and rocked on his heels before he spoke. "I'm the first person you told…except for the shrink."

I nodded, uncertain. His changing moods and conversational twists and turns started to annoy me.

"Thank you for telling me."

Huh? He made my head spin.

"I'm honored," he said, like I'd bestowed some great award.

Yet all I'd given him was the great, ugly burden of truth—and he was honored. Even though I thought he was crazy, warmth seeped in and began to fill the empty, aching place inside me.

He framed my face with his hands. "You deserved to be protected."

Stupid, pointless emotion clogged my throat. "Yeah, I did. But I'm not eight years old. I'm almost eighteen, and I can take care of myself."

I could tell he didn't like this, but he nodded reluctantly. "Yes, you can take care of yourself." He kissed my forehead. "He moved away?"

"Yes," I replied, withholding the fact that he'd moved back. And that he was practically famous. A powerful man. So, although I'd promised to be truthful, I withheld *this* truth. A lie of omission.

"Okay. It's just as well he moved, because if he still lived here, I'd probably kill him."

I know the sentiment was sincere, but Matt wouldn't really kill him. Maybe just beat the crap out of him, like he'd said earlier. Even that would be very, very bad.

We stared into each other's eyes, allowing the full weight of this evening to absorb into our hearts and minds, to become a part of our relationship.

I, Margaret Annabelle Bryant, welcomed, no *embraced*, my first real relationship. Biting the inside of my lip, I smiled.

We walked beside the lake, stopping occasionally to stare at the water, at the trees, at each other. Sometimes we kissed—tender kisses that left me feeling safe and protected...and cherished. Mostly we were content to just exist in our own quiet part of the world.

I thought maybe, just maybe, I hadn't burdened him with more than he could handle.

* * *

Tonight I appreciated not having a curfew. We pulled into my driveway well after 1:00 a.m., exhausted but secure in our growing relationship.

He walked me to the front door, and I sensed a new protectiveness as we kissed goodnight—not that I needed protecting. I'd been very clear about this. But still, it wasn't awful and maybe even kind of nice. He left reluctantly, after promising to pick me up for lunch the next day.

Long after he left, even with the dark tendrils of anger that hid deep inside me, happiness bubbled within, filling me with a sense of rightness, of contentment. I thought maybe I felt joy.

For sure, I reveled in a sense of accomplishment. I might still struggle at times with what had been done to me, but I knew—I *knew*—that today I had taken a huge and amazing step toward leaving the past behind me. I was in control of my bold new world.

A world that included Matt.

Chapter Nineteen

My dad died defending our country when I was little.
I barely remember him. In my favorite picture, he's
wearing his Army fatigues and holding me in his arms.
I like to think...

I like to think that if he hadn't died, he'd have protected
me all my life.

He was the strong one in our family.
 —Maggie's Journal

Matt and I spent a lot of time together over the next two weeks.
We met before school, ate lunch together, and often studied
together in the evening. He was kind, funny, smart...and he
was my boyfriend.

It was like a dream. Sometimes I couldn't quite believe it
was real. That this great guy was into *me*.

Tonight we were going out for dinner at a nice restaurant—a
real dress-up date. Matt said it was for our three week
anniversary. The big goof. Who celebrates three weeks? And

besides he was math challenged!

When I'd told him this, he just shrugged and said he'd counted the first great week, skipped the one off week, and counted the next two. Three. Well, I couldn't argue with that.

I peeked in the mirror one last time and grinned. Who celebrates three weeks? Me and my guy, that's who. My outfit was hot—black leggings, a short skirt, and knee-high black leather boots. An forest green silk sweater turned my eyes a nice blue-gray.

For a first fancy date, this would do.

The doorbell rang. I checked my phone. 6:30. Right on time.

Pleased that Mom had already left on her date for the evening, I grabbed my purse and hurried down the hall. I peeked through the peephole, and there he stood. My heart flip-flopped at the sight of him in gray dress pants and a navy blue long-sleeved shirt, his dark brown hair carefully combed except for that one stubborn lock that fell against his forehead.

Ba-boom. My guy.

I brushed my hair with my hand to make sure it lay smooth, and then opened the door.

His eyes lit in appreciation. "Hey." He smiled. "You look great."

Good grief! I could feel the heat of a blush rising in my cheeks. "Thanks. You, uh, look nice." Nice? Didn't even come close to describing his gorgeous, sexy self.

"Maggie?" He tilted his head, watching me watch him.

Yep. I was staring.

"Are you ready?" I asked and fought the urge to smack myself upside the head. "I mean, I'm ready." Shoving the door open so it almost whacked him, I stepped outside and locked the door behind me. Smooth was my middle name.

I spun around, and he captured me with one hand on each shoulder. Warmth seeped through my thin sweater. *Please, don't mention what a goober I'm being.* Seriously, I thought I'd die of embarrassment. But he simply leaned in and kissed me, slow and easy until I melted against him.

Then he stepped back and caught my hand in his. He walked me to the passenger side of his truck, waiting until I was inside before shutting the door. It was silly, really, because I was perfectly capable of getting in the car by myself—but it was nice, too.

He cranked up country music, and we rode in comfortable silence to the restaurant, hands clasped between us the entire way.

* * *

The hostess led the way through the Italian restaurant's fancy dining room. Soft lighting favored the customers' faces, so they glowed with contentment over the fine meals. And maybe they did. It smelled amazing.

Our table sat near the windows, with a view of an open air patio that consisted of golden stucco walls on three sides and an iron rail on the fourth that provided an expansive view of the hilly countryside. A full moon shone bright, filling the spacious area with magical light.

Magical light for a magical night.

Aargh! I tapped my fingers in annoyance at the sappy thought. This was so not me.

"Great, isn't it?" Matt wore a ridiculously big grin on his face.

I couldn't help but smile in return as I nodded.

A single red rose sat smack in the middle of our table. Actually, a red rose sat on every table, but our rose...well, it was perfect.

We were reading our menus when a beautiful woman entered the room. Heads turned—both male and female. Tall and slim, she wore a white suit. Only a confident woman wore white like that to an Italian restaurant. Too much red sauce. I was impressed. Her blond hair floated past her shoulders.

A little honey-haired girl, maybe first or second grade, held tight to the sophisticated lady's hand. She carried herself like a little princess, wearing a dark purple dress with cap sleeves and a tight fitting bodice. The skirt flowed out from her waist. It would fly out about her if she twirled.

Had I ever been that young? That innocent? For the first time that night, the bite of heartache intruded on my special night.

"You okay?" Matt touched my hand and studied my face. "She's about the age you were...when it happened?"

I actually kind of liked the way he mentioned it. Like it wasn't a taboo subject and we could talk about it if I wanted. I nodded but said nothing.

"Are you ready to order?"

Saved by the waitress, I picked up the menu. Tonight, our night, I didn't want to talk about my past.

* * *

Dinner tasted delicious, definitely living up to the wonderful aroma that filled the room. I took my last bites of chicken spiedini while Matt polished off his chicken parmesan. Good dinner, good company, an all around great night.

As Matt reviewed the dessert menu, a man's laughter drifted across the dining area, somehow distinguished from the voices of other patrons. The hair on the back of my neck stirred, and my gaze drew to a table on the other side of the room. Ice ran up my spine, then splintered throughout my body, until I sat frozen and fractured, my fingers permanently conformed to the handle of my fork.

Warren.

Chapter Twenty

Sometimes life just sucks. Get over it.
—Maggie's Journal

Warren Johnson, the monster, was here.

He stood next to a table of four, dressed in an expensive dark gray suit, chatting with the seated couples. I hadn't seen him in person since that day when Mom and I went to lunch for my fourteenth birthday.

I had, unfortunately, been subjected to numerous sightings of him on television and read too many articles about him in the paper. I also crossed paths with his nephew at school. The frequency with which life reminded me of his existence had convinced me I was prepared for this.

I was wrong.

A simmering anger brewed inside me. It started deep in my gut, like a stomach ache, and built until it was less a pain and more a power, dark and churning, demanding release. Emotion overflowed, and Warren reached back and rubbed his neck, glancing to the side, as if the hatred in my stare actually pierced him.

"Maggie?" Matt's voice summoned me from the dark place.

I turned my smoldering gaze his way. Rewinding the last seconds, I realized this wasn't the first time he'd called my name. His eyes widened. "Are you okay?"

I gave myself a mental shake. "Yeah, sorry. What did you say?" I refused—*refused*—to let Warren ruin our evening.

"I just wondered what you wanted for dessert." Matt set the menu in front of me.

Suddenly, the thought of dessert turned my stomach. "Mmmm, it's all good. How about creme brulee? Or maybe something chocolate? I can't decide."

"How about the molten chocolate cake for two? We can share." He reached over to take my hand in his.

Really, he was the best date ever. I knew this even with my lack of experience. "Okay," I responded, careful to keep my focus on him.

"Maybe after dinner we could…" He stopped talking, then continued, pointing to the far side of the room. "Wow, it's Warren Johnson."

My blood ran cold. That old saying took on new meaning as the white hot anger of a moment ago turned into ice cold shock, no, horror. My breath transformed, trapping painful shards of ice inside my throat.

Matt spoke Warren's name as if he were a celebrity. And since he'd just launched his campaign for county prosecutor, I guess he was.

Thank God I'd seen him earlier. Even so, only the years of practice controlling my emotions allowed me to casually turn my head in the direction Matt indicated.

"Did you know he played football for our high school? He was All State his senior year. Had more full ride offers than

106

anyone in the history of the school."

Hero worship. Unfreakingbelievable. I turned back to Matt, certain disbelief and horror were stamped all over my face. Matt didn't even notice, his gaze glued to Warren.

"He went to Notre Dame undergrad and Harvard law school. He's a legend! The biggest booster. He even talked to the team last year, and...he's coming over here. What..."

I peered back at Warren, and sure enough, he was headed toward us. The ice melted, a slow thaw that turned my stomach. The delicious chicken morphed into a thick, churning sludge. I struggled not to throw up my dinner...although perhaps if I aimed just right, I could deposit the spiedini down the front of Warren's expensive suit.

When he arrived at our table, he barely glanced my way, his one-hundred-watt charisma focused on Matt. "Matt McGuire! It's good to see you."

Matt shoved back his chair, beaming because his *hero* remembered him. He stood, and they shook hands.

"How's school? Keeping those grades up?" Warren ignored me.

Despite my best efforts, however, I could not tear my eyes from him. Who the hell did he think he was, intruding on my wonderful evening?

Invading my life again.

"Yes, sir."

You'd have thought Warren and Matt were best buddies. Matt beamed in the spotlight of Warren's attention.

"Why don't you contact my office tomorrow? We have a couple of internships for high school students. Tell them I recommended you."

"Yes, sir. Thank you."

Finally, Warren glanced at me and smiled. The slimy, no good pervert. "You've got yourself a fine young man here." He didn't acknowledge knowing me, but he didn't act like we'd never met either.

As if I were on autopilot, I returned his smile without intending to do so. Damn the years of controlling emotion and maintaining social niceties. He was doing this on purpose. I could read it in his eyes the moment he registered my fake smile and hate-filled eyes, and he realized I wasn't the clueless little teenager I'd been almost four years before.

He knew that I knew. If anything, his smile broadened. What was his game? My heart picked up pace. Didn't he know I could out him right now, this very minute?

The bastard. He was so confident, so sure of himself and me. He turned his attention back to Matt. "Actually, the hiring manager is in the back room with us. Can you talk for a minute? I'd like to introduce you."

"Well, sir, I'm with my...

"No, really it's fine," I insisted. *Sir*. I needed time. I needed to remember how to breathe. I needed not to throw up my dinner right here in the middle of this fancy dining room. "You go ahead."

The waitress walked up behind Matt.

"Are you sure?" my guy asked. He meant *are you sure it's okay if I meet the person who could give me a cool job*, but I heard *are you sure it's okay if I go hang out with my hero, the guy who abused you*.

I nodded, careful to ignore Warren completely. I was one step away from either losing my dinner or tossing my glass of ice water into his smug, lying face. Of the two, I'd prefer the water. Unfortunately, panic and all-consuming sickness further encroached on my anger.

I swallowed a scream of frustration. It tasted bitter. "I'll order our dessert while you're gone." My voice remained calm, very, very controlled.

Matt, oblivious, practically vibrated with excitement, and in that moment, I hated him, too. "I'll be right back."

I nodded in what I hoped passed for encouragement, and watched as my dream guy walked away with my worst nightmare.

I managed to order dessert before my throat started to close and my breathing picked up pace. The walls of the restaurant pressed in. Voices swirled and increased in volume.

I thrust my chair back so abruptly the couple at the next table startled. "Sorry," I muttered and pasted a smile on my face.

I forced myself to walk—not run—to the courtyard. Gulping a great breath of night air, I didn't stop until I'd reached the shadows of the far corner and grasped the metal rail with trembling hands.

An unseasonably warm breeze caressed my hot face. I stared at the night sky, breathing in, out, in, out, and battled to regain my composure. As my heart slowed, I turned to study the courtyard. Moonlight flooded the area, reflecting off the deep brown tile floor, casting shadows along the golden stucco walls. Gas lamps lit each corner. I catalogued each detail, gaining composure from the focus on small and mundane details.

I flopped down on a carved wooden bench, tilting my head back against the rough wall so I could search for constellations in the thousands of twinkling stars. Normally, I'd have found them beautiful, but tonight, they mocked my fleeting happiness.

No way in hell was I spending my summer listening to Matt sing the praises of Warren Johnson. *Asshole*. Warren, not Matt, although truthfully, I was pissed at Matt as well. Poor guy. I knew this wasn't his fault.

After I told Matt the truth, after he accepted what happened in my past, I'd thought that I, Maggie Bryant, who'd spent years in emotional hiding, finally had it all.

Turns out I had exactly nothing. Because no way could I tell Matt the truth about Warren. Matt's vow burned in my brain.

It's just as well he moved, because if he still lived here, I'd probably kill him.

I couldn't tell Matt, and I couldn't be in a relationship that included Warren, no matter how peripheral.

Warren was ruining my life…again.

Chapter Twenty-one

Once innocence is lost, you can never get it back.
  —Maggie's Journal

I needed to go back inside. Matt would wonder where I was, but I couldn't convince my legs to get moving. So I stared into the night and wondered how my life had gone so wrong. A whiff of spice and beer seemed to float in the air, turning my stomach. I shook my head, my imagination working overtime.

Movement near the entrance caught my eye. The little girl I'd seen earlier wandered into the enclosed courtyard. Her purple dress hugged her small shoulders and waist. The skirt flared out below her hips and drifted in graceful folds at her calves. Her honey-blond hair fell in waves midway down her back, shimmering against the rich color of her dress.

Oh yeah, she was definitely a little princess. Frowning, I searched behind her, but saw no one. What kind of mom left her child to wander alone? Didn't she know it wasn't safe?

I decided to keep an eye on her until her mom came for her. It gave me purpose, however fleeting.

She spun in the moonlight, her dress billowing about her, a

stark contrast against the golden walls. Despite the pain eating my insides, I smiled. I knew that skirt would fly.

Suddenly she stopped. Something near the gas light had caught her eye. She ran forward, her skirt flowing behind her, and skidded to a stop in front of the lamp to stare at the fluttering moths.

Following the flight of the closest moth, she raised her hands, little palms cupped, and tracked its path. Then, she snatched it out of the air and held it in her hands. She talked to it in hushed tones before walking to the rail and setting it free. Returning to the light, she repeated the process again and again.

The fourth time, something went wrong. She opened her hands at the rail, and the moth didn't take flight. She turned to me, her luminescent green eyes concerned. "It won't fly."

I hadn't realized she knew I was there.

I approached slowly and crouched down in front of her. "Let me see."

The little girl opened her palms wide. The moth fluttered in her palm, one of its wings slightly askew. She'd injured it.

Intensely aware of her hopeful eyes, I smiled. "I think this moth like bushes." Nodding my head toward an evergreen that had been pruned into an elegant spiral, I stood. We walked over, and she set the moth carefully on the bush.

The little girl's face lit up, and she grasped my fingers. "She's happy." I heard a hint of wistfulness in her voice.

"I think she is." I squeezed her hand gently in acknowledgement.

"Ashley," a woman's voice called from the terrace entrance. "It's time to go."

The little girl stiffened, her eyes on the moth.

I wanted to laugh. Clearly she had many more moths to

catch before she was ready to leave. Her hand slipped slowly from mine, her reluctance obvious.

"Come on, Ashley, let's go." A man's voice, deep, charming, unforgettable. Menacing in its sheer power to conceal betrayal and lies. My heart lodged in my throat, my hard-won composure disappearing in a flash.

The man sounded exactly like…

Warren.

A haunted look crossed Ashley's face. Or was that just me, projecting my own rioting feelings? She left my side, and I turned, praying it wasn't him, all the while certain it was.

Warren. His eyes bored into mine, daring me to speak, then he smiled and turned away. The elegant woman in the pristine white suit stood beside him. She took Ashley's small hand in hers and smiled at me, nodding her thanks. Warren grasped the little girl's other hand, and the three of them left the courtyard.

Where before the solitude had gradually comforted me, now silence smothered me. I followed as if in a trance. Stopping in the doorway, I watched the three of them weave in and out of the tables, stopping every few steps to greet well-wishers. Warren released the little girl's hand to share a hearty handshake, his palm coming back to rest on her shiny hair.

Finally, they reached the exit. They paused to put on their coats, and I thought for a moment that Ashley was going to turn back and wave goodbye. But Warren grabbed her hand, and they disappeared through the doors and into the night.

I stared after them until the uncomfortable sensation of being watched drew my attention. I'd completely forgotten about Matt. Oh yeah, I was an awesome date. It wasn't his fault, I reminded myself. He remained blissfully unaware he'd been consorting with the enemy.

113

Slipping between tables, I joined him. He tracked my every move—much as I had watched Ashley.

"Hey. Sorry I didn't see you come back."

He stood and pulled out my chair. "It's okay." His eyes searched my face. "Are you okay? You're a little pale."

How many times in our relationship would I be at this crossroads? Tell the truth, reveal my true emotions, the full scope of betrayal, or slip by with another white lie. The kind I despised telling him.

I tried for somewhere in the middle. "My stomach was feeling a little upset, so I went outside for some fresh air." Dessert had been delivered while we were away. A fabulous molten chocolate cake with ice cream and two spoons now sat in the center of the table. "I feel better now. This looks yummy." I forced enthusiasm into my voice. It did look yummy. I just wasn't hungry anymore.

He pulled out my chair. "I have an interview for an internship with the County Prosecutor's Office on Thursday."

I had nothing to say.

He sat across from me. "Hey, I'm sorry about stepping away."

"I told you it was okay." I really, really wanted to go home.

"I know, but…well, enough about the interview. Let's eat." He handed me a spoon, his excitement barely controlled.

Matt was having a fantastic night.

Remembering my vow from the day before not to let Warren control my life, I shoved the encounter, the internship, and the little girl out of my mind and tried to enjoy what was left of my date. I could do it. After all, hadn't I been compartmentalizing for years?

* * *

114

I thought I hid the undercurrent of tension pretty well, until Matt stopped me as I was about to unlock my front door.

"You're pulling away again."

I couldn't summon the energy to protest. He was right.

"Maggie," his voice, persistent, caring, tinged with a bit of frustration, grated my already frayed nerves.

"I just...I didn't feel well after dinner." This much was true. "I didn't want to ruin our evening." Also true.

He shoved his hands in his pockets. "I thought...I thought you could tell me anything. If you don't feel well, just tell me. Okay?"

I searched his eyes and saw only caring. When I nodded, he pulled his hands from his pockets and cupped my face. Laying his forehead against mine, he whispered, "You can tell me anything."

Anything except the truth. At best, the truth would destroy his chance of getting the internship, and the internship was a big deal. At worst, I'd be bailing him out of jail after he beat the crap out of the assistant county prosecutor.

I couldn't tell him the truth. And I feared I couldn't be normal, or as normal as I could be, if he didn't know the truth. I should break up with him. Again. But then Warren would win.

No matter what I did, I worried we'd both lose.

Chapter Twenty-two

The trick to survival is to compartmentalize. Put the things that bother you, the things you can't change, in a little box and never let them out.
—Maggie's Journal

For two days, the little girl haunted me. She studied with me on Sunday, followed me to school on Monday, entered each classroom. She joined me on the volleyball court during gym, her knowing green eyes boring into mine.

I thought maybe I was losing my mind.

At lunch time I'd toyed with calling Dr. Shirk, but she couldn't help me. This time I didn't need her to tell me what I already knew. The little girl was in danger.

If I reported him, what would happen? I'd recanted before. Would the authorities even believe me? Would anyone even care what happened to me ten years ago?

I had no proof of my abuse. I didn't know for sure he was abusing Ashley.

In two months, I'd be eighteen. After that, the child abuse hotline wouldn't take a call regarding my abuse. And truthfully,

I knew nothing about hers.

Head pounding, I hesitated outside Ms. Williams' room after school and considered my options. By the time I stepped into the doorway, my heart raced. She was alone. I swallowed hard and forced a greeting. "Ms. Williams?" Maybe she didn't have time to talk with me.

"Maggie." She smiled. "Did you forget something?"

"Uh, no."

She frowned. "You have the highest grade in the class, so I doubt you need help with homework."

I shook my head. "I just have a question."

I meant to say it casually, but must have failed, because as I approached her desk, Ms. Williams hesitated and then slowly closed her laptop.

"Would you like to sit?"

I shook my head. "No, no, that's okay." I sucked in a deep breath. "I have a friend." I hesitated. I'd planned what to say as I procrastinated outside the door, but still the words stuck in my throat.

She smiled, but the smile didn't quite reach her eyes. "You have a number of friends."

This was kind of her. I was a bit of a loner, and we both knew it. "Yes, but I mean I have a friend who's been...abused." Unexpected tears stung my eyes. I blinked in annoyance and pressed on. "She wants to report, but she's worried."

Ms. Williams reached out and pulled a chair from beside her desk. She patted the seat. "Please sit."

Responding to the pull of an adult who cared, I sat gingerly on the edge of the seat. "I only have a few minutes."

"Okay." She smiled reassuringly. "Why is she worried?"

Concerned that she somehow knew or at least suspected

the truth, I plunged forward. "She's afraid he'll hurt her mom. That her mom will be mad if she tells. That the other kids will talk about her." My eyes widened. Where had all of that come from? I was afraid Warren would hurt us, but the rest? It spilled out of nowhere—out of the part of my mind where I shoved the things I didn't want to think about.

"This sounds confusing."

"It is." I nodded. "She's confused."

"Is she being abused now?"

The word yes was on the tip of my tongue. I thought of Warren at the restaurant. Was I being abused? Physically, no. But the bastard continued to hurt me. And last night as I relived his visit to our table over and over again, I'd been certain. He was doing it on purpose.

I shook my head. "No, it happened when she was little. She wanted to tell then, but her mom didn't want her to tell. She—her mom—was afraid. Afraid of the abuser." Saying the words aloud made them more real, more painful. It made me wonder. Had Mom also been afraid of people knowing? Of being a bad mom? Of losing a guy who was a good boyfriend in her eyes, except for this one thing.

Unexpectedly, a memory flashed in my mind. My mom and me sitting on Grandma's swing. Ice cream dripping. An ugly blue-black circle around Mom's wrist. Had there been other bruises that I'd never seen?

"Maggie." Ms. Williams drew me back to the present. "She could come and talk to me. I could help."

"How?"

"I could call the hotline with her. We could make sure they know she's afraid of the abuser."

The desire to call warred with the need to run, until it

became too much. I jumped to my feet. "I need to go now. Thanks. I'll tell...my friend."

I thought I heard a quiet "Maggie" as I hustled out the door, but I kept going before she could call me back. Before she could accuse me of being the girl in my story.

Accuse. The tiny hammers tapped a rapid beat against my skull.

Ms. Williams had offered to help. Matt had offered to help. But neither of them really understood. Neither of them could actually do anything. In the end, it all fell on me.

* * *

Sleep eluded me for hours. I tossed and turned until well after midnight. When I finally slept, I woke often, trapped in a recurring dream.

A full moon lit the Italian courtyard with ethereal light. A little girl twirled on the patio, her dress floating about her knees and then falling in graceful folds, only to flare again when she sent the skirts spinning with her pirouette.

She halted at the sight of moths flitting by the light of the gas lamps.

"Ashley," her mom called, and she turned to leave. Was it my imagination, or did her shoulders sag slightly in defeat? Was it more than leaving her precious moths behind?

"Ashley." Warren's voice boomed with charm. He brushed his palm over her hair before taking her small hand in his large one, and the elegant trio walked toward the restaurant exit.

Unable to take my eyes off them, I followed at a distance.

A tall, painfully thin woman approached them. "Mr. Johnson, how are you? This must be the little beauty you told me about. She's

119

lovely."

Little beauty. *Vomit rose in my throat.*

As they wound their way to the door, heads turned at the sight of this handsome family. The woman tall, slender, and blond. The man who commanded the room with his presence. The little girl so beautiful and innocent.

"She's a little beauty," a man called from across the room.

"A little beauty," another voice echoed.

I didn't see who said it.

Warren nodded in acknowledgement. They didn't stop again until they reached the door, pausing to greet yet another well wisher.

When the conversation finished and Warren opened the door to leave, the little girl turned, her hand slipping from his. Across the crowded room, her eyes sought mine and held.

For a moment we simply stared—deeply, knowingly, hauntingly. The other diners faded away, sounds grew faint, even Warren dissolved into nothingness.

There was only me and the little girl. Ashley. She opened her mouth and although her words were quiet, they filled the large room, silencing all other noise.

"Say something," she demanded.

And I was the only one who heard.

Chapter Twenty-three

Someone has to say something.
—Maggie's Journal

I jerked upright. Sweat rolled down my temples. My heart raced as adrenaline surged through my body.

Say something.

The little girl's eyes bored into me. I tossed back the covers and paced across my room. Her eyes followed. I couldn't escape them.

Say something.

I didn't want to know. I didn't want to know.

I.

…..Did.

…..……..Not.

…..……..……..Want.

…..……..……..……..To.

…..……..……..……..……..Know.

Damn it!

I slammed my palms against the wall, and then froze, listening for my mom. Nope. Nothing.

All the dreams I couldn't remember and this one remained as clear as if I'd just lived it.

As much as I hated it, I had no choice. Although it was only 3:00 a.m., I grabbed my laptop and climbed back in bed. Sliding under the covers, with Kitty tucked at my side, I googled him.

That asshole, Warren Pervert Johnson.

I found his address, discovered he was coaching basketball at the community center, found his new girlfriend on Facebook and saw pictures of the three of them. The woman and the girl—and Warren.

I studied picture after picture of Ashley. Her mom posted *a lot* of pictures.

Clicking on one, I scrutinized every detail. Adorable in a pink shirt with a silver rhinestone cat on the front, she posed for the camera. She'd lifted one foot in the air and despite the seriousness of my task, I bit back a smile. Her purple and pink tennis shoes featured matching silver sparkles.

The caption below the picture read: *Ashley shows off her cat's 54 sparkles—and ten more on each shoe. She counted them all! Second day of second grade.*

Was he abusing the little girl? She'd seemed happy enough at the restaurant, but I knew appearances weren't always true. The mom and little girl could have been me and my mom ten years ago.

I fought the truth even as it stared back at me, packaged in sweetness and glittering stones. As much as I wanted to ignore it, Warren appeared to have a type. And if he had a type...

Maybe it was just me, my inner voice argued, self-preservation at its finest. Because then it didn't matter if I did anything.

If I did nothing.

Maybe I was the only one. Maybe it had been just me.

I'd always thought it had been me. Something about me. Somehow deep inside, my fault.

Ohmygod. Ohmygod. I sucked in a desperate breath.

In.

Out.

In.

Out.

I forced myself to calm, to play my counselor's voice in my head. *Not your fault. Not your fault.* The spinning chaos in my brain slowly calmed.

Hell no, it wasn't my fault.

But...maybe *he'd* learned from the experience. He hadn't touched me again. Maybe even though I recanted, the report had scared him.

But...I knew the recidivism rate was high. Recidivism. A word I wished I didn't know the meaning of. High recidivism rate equaled likely to repeat. We'd learned this in class. But I'd never thought it applied to *him.*

Why had I never considered this?

I can't control everything. I can't control his behavior.

I shoved my laptop aside and clutched Kitty, rocking back and forth as I confronted my options. I was in a good place. A *good* place! I'd earned this place. *I deserved this place.* The world had dealt me a crappy hand, and I hadn't folded.

I'd put the past in the past. I was normal, mostly. I made good grades. I was headed for college. I had a boyfriend. I had for maybe the first time in a long, long time that thing other people took for granted. I had...

Happiness.

But, my annoying, preachy conscience argued, that wonderful future I'd fought for, that happiness, that bright shiny future—it was all about me.

Could I live with that?

Escape the past or confront it and risk my hard-won new world?

If I told, could I still be happy? If I didn't, could I ever be whole?

To report or not report? That was the question. And I knew which was nobler.

I knew.

Damn it!

Kitty and I huddled under the covers until sun beams broke around the sides of my window shade, signaling the coming of day.

There was nowhere to hide from the harsh and unyielding light of truth.

* * *

I'd confronted my past, confronted my choices. Now it was time to confront my mom. I wiped sweaty hands on my jeans and marched into the kitchen.

"Mom?" My voice rang more harshly than I'd intended, filled to overflowing with the resolve I'd struggled to achieve.

"Hi, honey. How did you sleep?" She took a final sip of coffee, grabbed her leather computer bag from the counter, and slung it over her shoulder. She'd dressed with care in a tailored cream suit and pale, peach silk blouse. Her dark hair hung loose and shiny, cropped at her chin.

I almost regretted ruining her day. Almost.

"Fine," I said. Well, that was a lie, but she didn't need to know how I'd tossed and turned over my decision. "I need to talk to you."

"Oh, Maggie, I'm sorry. I have to get to work early. Then I have a dinner date with Marvin." Mom blushed at the sound of his name.

I'd only met Marvin once. Although he actually seemed like a decent guy, right now ruining his date with my mom didn't make my list of concerns. "It can't wait."

Mom chewed her lip, checked her watch and then sighed. "All right." Annoyance crept into her voice. "Be quick."

I wound a strand of hair around my finger. I'd rehearsed this a hundred times, and still I couldn't find the words. My tough girl approach had lasted all of three minutes. That didn't mean I wasn't still determined. I could do this.

"Maggie, I don't have time for this."

Breathing deeply, I blurted, "I'm going to report Warren again. And this time I won't recant."

The air in the kitchen contracted, sucking out the oxygen, making it impossible to breathe.

Mom's face drained of color. She groped blindly for the chair, clutching the back to steady herself.

"Honey, we talked about this when you finished therapy last time. It's best to put this behind you. If you need to go back to therapy, that's fine."

Yes, I probably needed more therapy. Hell, once I reported I would for sure need more therapy. Because I was well aware my life might just fall completely and irrevocably apart.

Irrevocably. Vocabulary word, AP English.

Irrevocable. *Not able to be changed or reversed.*

In other words, no freakin' way out.

Mom retained her death grip on the polished oak and stared at me.

"I might need therapy," I admitted. "But that's separate from reporting Warren."

"You don't know what you're saying." She shoved the chair into the table and tucked her hair behind her ear.

Like me, she played with her hair when nervous, and in that moment, I hated it. Hated any sign that I was like her. I took an angry step toward the door, and then forced myself to stop and face her. "He shouldn't be able to get away with what he did to me. And he needs to be stopped so he can't...so he can't keep hurting little girls."

I waited, fists clenched at my sides.

For a long moment she said nothing, staring at me. Then, color flooded back to her cheeks. "He's a dangerous, powerful man. People won't believe you."

You recanted before. She didn't say the words, but we both heard them loud and clear. And we both knew she was to blame. Screw that. She wasn't telling me anything I hadn't already considered.

"Are you going to support me or not? I can do it without you, but I'd prefer to have you with me." I spoke slowly, controlling my anger, keeping my voice calm. I wanted her to see that I was committed to my choice.

Mom's bottom lip wavered. I saw, not for the first time, or the second, or even the last, that I, the child, was the adult in the room. I was the stronger person, the one who had to make sure we did the right thing.

Mom raised her chin. "I need to go. I need time to think about it. I..." She snatched her keys from the counter and brushed past me on her way to the door. I swear she flinched when she touched me. She opened the door and paused. Her eyes wide and worried, she whispered. "You have no idea

126

how this could destroy us." Then she slipped out of the house, running from me and the truth. Her final words carried from the porch just before the door slammed closed. "We'll talk tonight."

Tonight it would be too late for talk.

Chapter Twenty-four

The problem with compartmentalizing? If you're not careful, eventually you end up with Pandora's box.
   —Maggie's Journal

Minutes ticked by as I remained rooted to my spot in the kitchen, searching for the confidence to take the next step. Trying not to think about Mom. Had I really expected her to support me? I wanted to say no, but deep inside I couldn't deny that stupid, niggling optimism that whispered, "Maybe this time she'll take your side."

It was time.

I searched my phone for the Children's Division hotline. My hand trembled as I tapped the call link. My heart pounded in my ears.

The number popped up on my screen and gave me two options: *Cancel* or *Call.*

Ba-boom, ba-boom, ba-boom. I wished my heart would shut the hell up. I needed to actually hear the person when they answered. My thumb hovered over the options. Cancel or Call.

Cancel or...

Sweet Caroline, our school's football halftime theme song, blared from my phone. I jerked and nearly dropped it. The call was from Matt.

A combination of relief and frustration filled me. I had been about to select call. Really!

Ignoring Matt, I grabbed a piece of paper, wrote the number down, and crammed it into my pocket. I didn't know how long the call would take anyway. Better to call later. I slung my backpack over my shoulder and headed out.

When I was eight years old, I never actually made the decision to report. I confided in a friend, she told her mom, who told the teacher, and the teacher reported.

Now, *I* had decided.

And I was learning the hard way that deciding to report and actually reporting were two very different things.

* * *

I must have sped on the way to school, because I arrived twenty minutes before first hour and backed into my parking spot. Glancing at my phone, I saw the voicemail notification.

Matt. Missed call

Matt. Voicemail.

I shoved my phone into my pocket, slung my backpack over my shoulder, and headed toward the courtyard entrance at the back of the school. As I drew near, I saw him. Matt. Waiting on a bench in a quiet part of the courtyard, gorgeous as always in jeans, a dark green pullover and his letter jacket. *My guy.*

He stood as I neared, a big smile on his face. "You got my message." Leaning forward, he kissed me.

129

"I, uh—" A quick *yes* lie almost passed my lips, but I stopped myself. I wasn't the best girlfriend, that was for sure. But I'd promised myself to be an honest one, and except for my lie of omission, I was doing pretty well. I shook my head. "I'm sorry, I just saw the voicemail. I was going to listen inside."

"No problem. I just wanted to talk with you this morning." He overflowed with excitement.

Poor guy. He had no idea.

He shifted his feet. Despite my bigger issues, my curiosity piqued. What could make the normally unflappable Matt nervous?

He sucked in a breath. I realized he'd been holding one hand behind his back the entire time. "Would you do me the honor of being my date to Homecoming?" He whipped out the hidden hand to reveal a perfect red rose. I stared. The rose stood tall in his hand, a rich, glossy bud, just beginning to spread its petals.

"Maggie?" A gentle humor filled his voice. "It's for you."

"Oh, yes. It's beautiful." I took the rose carefully from his hand and then realized there was no need for caution. He'd removed all of the thorns. "It's beautiful," I repeated, my lips curving slightly. My heart fluttered and then dropped to land with a thud in my gut.

He stepped closer. His eyes searched mine. "And Homecoming?"

I should have been over-the-moon excited. Instead, my stomach churned. I hadn't made the call this morning, but I would make it. There was no turning back, and I knew it.

I hadn't consulted Matt, could not have consulted him any more than I had consulted my mom. This decision was on me. But it impacted him. I wasn't naive enough to believe I could report and there would be no repercussions, that people wouldn't find out. I wouldn't blame him if he wanted to run the other way.

"We need to talk." I clutched the stem, holding the rose close to my chest.

A crease wrinkled his brow, and I fought the urge to smooth it with my free hand. Now was not the time for touching.

"If you don't want to go, that's okay. We can do something else."

"No, that's not it. It's..." My voice faded as I struggled to find the right words. This was as difficult as revealing the truth about my abuse. Telling him I planned to report made the repercussions more real. Took me one step closer to the facts of my abuse being public. Common knowledge.

Matt's face fell. "Oh."

He knew me so well. He knew I had to tell, and he was disappointed. Even though I'd expected him to bail, the harsh reality hurt.

Huh? I wanted to bang my head on the stone bench. He had no way of knowing what I was going to say, no warning of what was to come. I...

"You're breaking up with me." Pain seeped through his monotone response, interrupting my internal rant.

What?! That wasn't it at all. "No...no! It's not that." I rambled. "God, no. I thought you were breaking up with me."

Relief and confusion flooded his handsome features. He tilted his head to the right. "I don't...I just asked you to Homecoming. How is that me breaking up with you?"

Poor Matt. No wonder he was confused. Again. By me.

The wind kicked up, and the rose's delicate aroma danced on the breeze. My beautiful, thornless rose. "I made a decision last night. I don't want to break up, but my choice will probably impact you." I knew it would.

Matt reached out and clasped my free hand in his. "Okay, then, what is it?"

I searched his eyes. All I saw was acceptance. And caring. I was so lucky.

Now I was going to risk throwing it all away. Through no fault of my own. Life was freakin' unfair. But then, I'd known that for years. I clutched his hand and struggled to push the words past the pain in my heart.

"I'm going to report the guy who abused me. Soon. This week." Today, but I didn't want to tell him that, wanted to lessen any urgency he might feel to support me—or convince me not to do it. "It's my problem. You didn't sign on for this."

He said nothing.

All of my thoughts tumbled out in a rush. "It'll be big news. I'm seventeen so my name should be kept private, but I'll be eighteen in a couple of months." His arrogant nephew went to our school. One way or another, people would know. "And he's...powerful." I wasn't ready to tell him everything yet. Not here in the courtyard. And I wanted him to have a shot at the internship before Warren found out.

Matt remained silent.

"I have to assume word will get out. Everyone respects him. People might not believe me." I repeated my mom's words. They'd hurt, but they'd also been true. "I recanted before."

"Maggie..."

"I'm not ready to tell you who he is. Not yet. Please don't ask me." I searched his face. "I understand if you want to ask someone else, someone, well, someone without humongous issues." Someone normal. I stared at my boots. "Someone..."

CHAPTER TWENTY-FOUR

"Maggie," he interjected again.

I stopped talking and, biting my lower lip, met his eyes.

"You're breaking my hand."

Mortified, I loosened my hold and tried to pull back. He held me tight in a gentle but firm grip.

"You should report." He lowered his head and brushed my lips with his. "I'm here for you. Whatever you need."

Matt was in. He was all in. Tears threatened, and my emotions ping-ponged from one extreme to another.

"Will you go to Homecoming with me?" Surprised by his casual attitude, a little annoyed by it honestly, I started to jerk away. But instead, something in his voice stopped me. I considered him closely for the first time since I told him I would report. Despite his smile, the tic was back in his jaw.

My heart broke. I knew that fake smile. I'd perfected it. And now I'd spread it to Matt like a virus for which there's no cure. I dug my nails into my palm and offered the only medicine I had to make it better. "Yes, I'd love to go to Homecoming." Fear that I'd damaged him irreparably shadowed the moment.

He nodded, an indication that he heard me. He stared at a spot over my shoulder, then jerked his eyes back to mine and blurted, "I want to be with you when you make the call."

"No." My response was automatic. I didn't need him there for the call. Actually, I needed him *not* there. "But thank you. I need to do this myself." Despite the fact that we were in the courtyard where other students could see us, I flung my arms around his neck. "I'm sorry," I whispered. "Sorry to put you through this."

He held me close, crushing the rose between us, then tilted his head to stare into my eyes. "Don't apologize again. This isn't your fault."

"I know, but it feels like it anyway." I stepped back, increasingly uncomfortable with the public display of affection.

"You told me he's powerful. That everyone loves him." Although no students lingered nearby, he kept his voice low.

I could feel our past conversations spinning through his mind.

"He's here isn't he? He never moved," Matt spoke with certainty.

I didn't want him believing that I'd lied. "No, he did move." I offered an apologetic half smile. "But he moved back."

He nodded. He'd already guessed the truth. "Tell me…"

Shaking my head, I placed my hand on his chest. "I will tell you. Just not here. Soon." After I'd reported. After he'd aced his interview.

"Are you okay? Are you scared?" He covered my hand with his.

I shook my head. "No, I'm fine. Really, don't worry."

I was doing enough of that for both of us.

Chapter Twenty-five

I am in control. I can do this.
—Maggie's Journal

Matt had offered to help make the call, but I'd said no. *No, thank you.* I wanted to do it myself.

But in the end, I needed help after all.

"Ms. Williams?" I stood in the doorway to her classroom. The rest of the class had escaped into the halls five minutes before when the dismissal bell rang.

"Maggie." She paused, observing me closely. "Is everything okay?

Instead of answering, I stepped inside and shut the classroom door. I hesitated, my hand strangely reluctant to release the knob—as if my fingers had a life of their own.

Yanking free, I trudged up the aisle and stopped in front of Ms. Williams' desk.

Her brow creased, and then her eyes widened as if she sensed the magnitude of this moment. The moment where everything changed. Because once I told her, there was no going back. I'd done enough research to know that she'd be required to report.

Stopping in front of her desk, I clenched my hands together in a tight knot. Butterflies—and not the good kind—took flight in my stomach.

"Maggie?" Her eyes searched mine.

I was pretty sure she was remembering our earlier conversation. The one about my *friend*.

Silence grew. Awkward and annoying. To hell with it, I plunged in. "I need to call the child abuse hotline. You said you'd help...me." Because I wasn't here for a friend or to *tell* Ms. Williams anything. I was here to make a report.

She nodded as if she wasn't surprised, then stood, walked around the desk and pulled me into a hug. "I'm glad you asked me." She stepped back and again she searched my face. "Do you want to do it now?"

I nodded.

She pulled her chair around the side of her desk, so we were each sitting on one side of the corner. "Do you want to hold the phone, or should I put it on speaker?"

I toyed with the phone chord. "Speaker."

"Okay."

"Okay."

I reached in my pocket, pulled out the folded piece of paper. Carefully, I smoothed the creases against the flat surface of her desk. "I have the number." It was time. My palms grew damp. I froze.

When I continued to stare at the number, she placed her hand over mine and just waited, giving me time. My heart raced. I squared my shoulders and dialed.

I startled when the ringing of a phone blared out from the speaker. Ms. Williams adjusted the volume down just as a no nonsense recording answered. "You've reached the Missouri Child Abuse Hotline. If the child you're calling about is in immediate danger or living in a meth lab, hang up and dial 911, then call us back. If the child is in danger of abuse in the next 24 hours, press 1, for all other calls, press 2."

I thought about the little girl. Even though I couldn't report her abuse, because truthfully, I didn't know anything about her, I still *knew*.

I pressed 1.

Ms. Williams gave my hand a squeeze.

The phone rang twice. "Hi, this is Kim with the Missouri Child Abuse Hotline. Are you calling to report the abuse of a child?"

"Yes."

"What is the child's name?"

My throat threatened to close, cutting off my ability to speak. "Ma'am?"

I took a deep breath and forced out the words. "Margaret Annabelle Bryant." Who'd have thought simply saying my name would require that much strength? I continued to answer questions, giving her my age, birthday, address and phone number. My age when I was abused...my age today.

"What is the name of the perpetrator?"

I stared at the phone. A voice with no face. Cold plastic in which I was placing my trust...and my truth.

"Warren Johnson."

At the mention of his name, Ms. Williams gasped, a tiny sound but I heard it. I had to give Kim credit, she continued as if I hadn't mentioned a man who was praised daily in the news. I told her they could find him at the county prosecutor's office. Again, she didn't hesitate. Maybe in her career, she'd heard it all.

The call took fifteen minutes. Once my initial panic passed, I told her everything in monotone. *Just the facts ma'am.* What had happened to me. How my mom convinced me to recant. My mom's concerns that Warren would find a way to hurt us for revealing his crimes.

My fear that he was abusing the little girl from the restaurant. Ashley. I provided her last name. Let Kim know I'd discovered it on Facebook.

Although you can make anonymous calls to the hotline, I'd told her that I was Margaret Annabelle Bryant. I had to tell her. I needed her to take me seriously. I needed *the system* to know I was recanting my recant.

The call drained every ounce of energy from my body. Ms. Williams and I sat in shared anticipation as Kim put me on hold. She returned in less than a minute.

"Maggie, thank you for calling. This call constitutes a credible suspicion of child abuse under Missouri Law and will be referred to the Jackson County Office of Investigation. An employee will contact you for more information." She gave me my case number.

After she hung up, the dial tone blared from the speaker until Ms. Williams pressed the disconnect button.

We both stared at the now silent phone. Nerves rushed in to fill my energy void. My foot tapped against the floor.

Ms. Williams spoke first. "It's very, very unusual for someone accused to retaliate. It hurts their case with the police."

Biting my lip, I agreed. "I know. My shrink and I have talked about it. But still, he's a powerful man. Charming—and a freakin' pervert."

Worry stamped a frown on her normally smiley face. "Do you need anything? Will your mom be home?" She didn't say what we were both thinking. It wouldn't be long until Warren found out.

"No, I'm good. I have volleyball practice, and then my mom will be home." She'd be home late. After her date with Marvin. And when she found out I'd already reported? She'd be...mad? Scared? Hysterical? I dreaded finding out, almost more than I'd dreaded the call.

I'd made the call. And despite having to tell my mom, regardless of the potential fallout, in that moment I felt good. Powerful. I wasn't afraid.

Not then, at least.

* * *

I arrived at practice ten minutes late and ran the required laps, making no excuses. Practice flew by—too quickly, because I had no desire to go home and confront Mom.

When I finally pulled into my driveway, I was exhausted. I sat there, knowing Mom wasn't home yet, but reluctant to go in anyway.

A strange car pulled up next to me. A red SUV with tinted windows that I'd seen parked on our street when I turned in. *Oh damn.* What if Warren had found out already? I fumbled for my phone, dropping it to the floor. As I scrambled to get it, I heard a door slam shut. My heart leapt into my throat.

I clenched the phone and straightened in the seat, prepared to dial 911. A second car pulled in behind me. I hit the 9 before I recognized...Matt?

Thank God, thank God. I threw my door open and forced

myself to walk, not run, to his car.

"Hey, Maggie…" His eyes widened as they settled on my face. "What's wrong?"

The door to the SUV opened and a young guy hopped out, a friendly smile on his face.

"Matt. Dude, I've been waiting."

"Sorry I ran late. Maggie, this is my cousin, Ryan. Ryan, Maggie. He works part time for a security company."

He what? I slugged Matt's arm for the second time in one week. Matt—or this situation, I wasn't sure which—drove me crazy. I was not a violent person.

"Ouch," he pretend-protested. "What's that for?"

"I didn't know who he was. He followed me."

Instead of apologizing, Matt's eyes narrowed. "You're the most frustrating person." His voice dropped to a whisper. "I asked if you were scared, if you needed help."

I shrugged. "I'm not scared."

Matt raised his eyebrows in obvious disbelief.

I sighed. I had made a promise to myself to be truthful. "Yeah, well, I didn't know I was going to be scared."

"You can count on me."

"I know." I glared at him and emphasized my point. "I hadn't *planned* on being scared. I…"

Before I could say anything else, Ryan joined us. "I can't install anything without the homeowner's approval." He frowned. "Sorry."

"That's fine. Just tell us what you'd do."

I let Matt do the talking. I had no idea what was going on.

"You say it's her mom's old boyfriend who's been causing grief?" Ryan asked.

I jerked my head his direction. He knew?

CHAPTER TWENTY-FIVE

Matt leaned down and whispered, "I made it up."

I fought the urge to giggle hysterically. He had no idea.

"Yes," Matt told Ryan. "We're afraid he'll try to break in."

"Okay, so you'll need a motion sensitive camera on the front that captures anyone coming up to the house. And one in the back." He talked us through the plan. Something about IPs and NVRs and continuous something or others.

Normally, I'm tech savvy, but today, my mind spun in an unending loop with thoughts of reporting, telling my mom, Matt thinking he could make decisions for me. Technology ranked low on my list of priorities.

"We need sound," Matt said.

"Sound? That's more expensive."

"That's fine," Matt answered as if price wasn't a blip on his radar.

"Wait a minute." I found my voice. "You can't just..."

Matt placed one finger gently against my lips. "It's a birthday present."

My eyes narrowed. *Stupid boyfriend.* He didn't even know my birthday—although I guess I had mentioned turning eighteen soon. I wanted to protest that I didn't need his help, but unfamiliar, unwanted emotion clogged my throat.

He was watching out for me. I swallowed the lump of mushiness. For so long, I'd had only me.

"'scuse me." Ryan's voice intruded as if from a distance.

I turned and found him studying us like bugs under a microscope.

"I'll get what we need and install it Saturday. Sorry I can't do it sooner."

"My mom will never sign for this," I blurted.

Matt squeezed my hand. He and Ryan did some guy

communication thing with their eyes.

Ryan nodded. "I won't be on the clock then. It'll just be friends helping friends."

A horn honked, and we spun to face the street, jerking as if we'd been caught breaking the law with our *clandestine security installation*. My urge to giggle died when I saw it was Mom. She must have cancelled her date. Ryan's SUV blocked her path to the garage.

"Thank you. Both of you. But you need to go. I...I need to talk to my mom." I felt Matt stiffen and saw the question in his eyes. He wanted to know the identity of my abuser, wanted to know so he could keep me safe.

Mom honked again. Now wasn't the time to tell him.

Chapter Twenty-six

I recanted because my mom told me to. What else is there to say? She told me to recant.

And I was a good little girl.
  —Maggie's Journal

As Matt and Ryan backed out of the driveway, I entered the house. My earlier exhaustion disappeared, and I zipped around, propelled by nervous energy. Yanking open the refrigerator door, I pulled out leftover meatloaf and vegetables and shoved them in the microwave. While they nuked, I set the table and poured two glasses of milk. I'd never served a quicker meal.

The door from the garage opened and shut.

"Maggie." Mom sighed, her voice both tentative and frustrated. It only added to the buzz of energy that had replaced my earlier exhaustion. What business did she have sounding exasperated with me?

The microwave dinged.

"Dinner's ready." I avoided her eyes. Instead, I whipped the food out and plopped it on the table. Then I sat and shoveled a bite into my mouth.

"Maggie, we need to talk…"

And suddenly I couldn't do it. Not right now. Anger poured through every cell of my body. Anger that I hadn't slept last night, that I'd had trouble focusing in class, that I'd been ridiculously scared by Matt's cousin who was trying to do something nice for me.

Anger at my mom. It clawed at my gut, rage growing until it threatened to explode. I shoved my chair back and grabbed my backpack and plate. "I have a lot of homework tonight. Going to eat in my room," I called over my shoulder and fled down the hall.

I pushed my bedroom door closed with my foot and leaned back against the wood. Breaths came hard, as if I'd run a long distance. I shut my eyes and refused to fall apart.

When I opened my eyes and straightened, the plate in my hand tipped and meatloaf slid toward the floor. I dropped my backpack and lunged with my free hand, catching the slippery mass while my fork and most of the mixed vegetables rained down onto my carpet.

The perfect ending to my already difficult day.

I ate a couple of big bites of meatloaf right out of my hand, then put the remaining food on the plate and washed up using my water bottle and a shirt from the dirty clothes. No way I was braving the hall—and my mom—to wash my hands in the bathroom.

Then I made myself comfortable on the bed and studied. Two hours later, I wrapped up my last subject just as a knock sounded at my door. Soft, like the person asking to enter wanted to be anywhere but here.

Mom.

"Come in." I sucked in air and blew it out hard.

Mom entered. She just stood there, twisting her hands. This was going to be ugly, and I'm pretty sure we both knew it.

"I'm sorry." Mom surprised me by opening the conversation with an apology. "I know I let you down. I swear, I didn't know. I didn't know what he was doing."

Would I ever be able to hear this excuse without the answering *you should have known* running through my brain?

She took a step closer. "I'm worried about you. Yes, I have my own fears, but mostly I'm worried about you."

Another step placed her next to my bed. Her hand reached out, almost touching me. But it stopped short and fell, useless, to her side. "Your life is so good now. Your grades are great. You're starting on the varsity team. You have a wonderful boyfriend. One I'd like to get to know some day. You're happy. Why would you want to risk that?"

What was I supposed to say? I'd thought through all of these things. And in the end, I'd chosen the only option I could live with.

Pounding started at my temples. I just wanted her to shut up.

"Maggie, Warren is a very dangerous man. He can be violent. I know he never hurt you..." Her voice drifted off when I shot a hate-filled glare her way. "Honey, I mean he never hurt you physica—damn it, Maggie! He can be a violent man."

She threw her hands up in the air and paced to the dresser where she picked up my dinner plate. "You understand what I'm trying to say. And he has friends. If he doesn't hurt us physically, he can turn people against us. He can spread lies about you. He's a powerful, respected man." Her voice dropped to a pained whisper. "You recanted."

Because you told me to. The words hung unspoken in the air between us. Ugly. Hurtful. True.

"I'm just asking you to think about it." She returned to the bed and leaned down to kiss my forehead. She lingered as if hoping for a response, but I had nothing for her. "I love you," she choked out and then walked back to the door.

She paused with her back to me and then turned around. Her eyes glistened. "I want what's best for you. Not just what's easiest for me." She studied my carpet before addressing me again. "There's no option that's easy."

When she started to leave, I stopped her. "I already made the call. I reported him. Again."

I thought her hand trembled on the door knob. I couldn't be sure.

"I saw him when Matt and I went out to dinner. He's with another woman who has a little girl." I wanted to be all calm and matter of fact, but my voice shook.

The ugly possibilities filled the room, weighing us down. Mom's shoulders slumped, and she nodded without turning around. She brushed her free hand across her eyes. "Okay then," she whispered.

I didn't feel bad for her. It was overwhelming enough dealing with my own roller coaster emotions.

She left the room, pulling the door shut behind her.

Chapter Twenty-seven

I learned at an early age that the only person I could count on was me.
  —Maggie's Journal

My timing was either very good or very bad, depending on my point of view. Mom left for Chicago early the next morning for two days of meetings.

Mostly when Mom left, I felt relief. Her absence gave us both much needed space, but it also left me alone. No big deal normally. I'd been staying alone overnight when Mom traveled since I was sixteen.

School passed in a blur. Matt's concerned eyes tracked my every move when we saw each other. If he didn't watch it, I was going to slug his arm again.

After practice, I jogged to my car. My phone vibrated as I slung my backpack inside.

Mom.

"Hi." If my response sounded abrupt, well, it was what it was.

"Maggie, it's Mom."

She always said that, even though she knew phones had this thing called *caller ID*. Jeesh!

"Listen, if you want to have Matt or one of your friends stay over tonight, that's okay. I'll be back late tomorrow night. I'm sorry I had to leave. This trip was important." Her words rushed out, flustered, worried.

"I'm fine, Mom. The house is locked up, and he's not going to do anything." I prayed hourly that this was true.

Okay, the truth? My worry increased in comparison with how long it had been since I reported. The more time, the more likely Warren knew.

And when Warren found out…well, I didn't want to be a sitting duck in case he decided to come after me.

On the way home, I detoured to our local drug store and picked up a few things I didn't need—soda, chips, napkins, straws—before tossing in my real objective. Pepper spray. As if adding the other items somehow made the pepper spray less conspicuous.

Dumping my items on the counter, I nudged the napkins until they covered the spray, then peeked over my shoulder to make sure no one I knew watched. I could just hear one of my mom's busybody friends saying *Maggie Bryant, why in the world are you buying pepper spray?*

I held my breath as the checkout guy scanned my items. The soda, the napkins, the pepper spray…

I held my breath, picturing him hitting the intercom. "Price check on pepper spray. Price check on pepper spray." Sometimes I really hated my overactive imagination.

The pepper spray rang up without a hitch. The guy held it in his hand, then glanced at me, the spray hovering over the bag.

Drop it in. Drop it in. Drop it...

"You know we have pink pepper spray. Just below this gray one."

Really? Pink?

"Do I look like a pink kind of girl?" I snapped. Pink reminded me of frilly curtains and princess rooms—and the need for pepper spray.

He shrugged, unimpressed by my outburst, and dropped it into the bag.

Forty-five minutes after Mom called, locked safely in our house, pepper spray secure in my pocket, I at last let down my guard. I felt silly being so cautious. After all, it had only been a little over twenty-four hours since I reported. And I wasn't in danger of being abused. My case probably wasn't even a priority, which meant it couldn't have come to Warren's attention yet. Right?

Still, I wished I'd waited until Ryan had installed those stupid security cameras I pretended I didn't need. I read the pepper spray instructions. Twice.

The doorbell rang. My pulse shot into overdrive.

It could be anybody. Next door neighbor, Girl Scouts, Jehovah's Witness.

Warren.

I checked my watch. I'd made the call exactly twenty-seven hours and fifteen minutes before. Jamming my hand into my pocket, I grabbed the pepper spray. I shook my head and rolled my shoulders to loosen up. Surely I'd open the door and discover a group of enthusiastic Girl Scouts. They'd stalked the neighborhood just yesterday.

Forcing myself to walk calmly to the entryway, I peeked out the tiny window and, resigned, opened the damned door.

"Would you like to buy some Girl Scout cookies?" Two little girls grinned at me. Their moms stood at the curb, keeping watch.

See. Girl Scouts.

I bought Thin Mints, locked up, and camped out at the kitchen table with homework for company.

Matt called a couple of times after he got off work. He wanted to come over, but I insisted I was fine. Besides, he had his interview with the County Prosecutor's office the next day. Until he'd clinched the interview, I planned to avoid him without it being obvious I was avoiding him.

In the midst of all the uncertainty haunting me, I could control this. I could protect Matt—at least for now.

Regardless of what happened with Warren, this internship was a great opportunity. So, I kept the conversations short, told him I was busy studying, and thanked him for calling.

It was a long night. and I really wished he was here.

* * *

The next morning, I learned that I, in fact, lacked the skills for inconspicuously avoiding Matt, because he cornered me before school.

"Maggie, what's going on? I'm worried." Concern marked his brow.

"I just have a lot of homework this week—"

He cut off my lame excuse. "You always have a lot of homework, don't—"

I gave him a quick peck on the lips. Both touched and annoyed that he knew me this well. "I promise to tell you everything tonight. When you get off work." After you finish

150

the interview.

I started to pull back, but he placed his hands on my hips and drew me forward. Right there in the school hall.

"You promise?"

"I promise." My stomach flipped. I'd promised, and I dreaded keeping it.

Warren was his hero.

Chapter Twenty-eight

*When Pandora's box opens, is it better to run or stand
your ground?*
  —Maggie's Journal

It was after dark when I pulled into the driveway. Practice had
run late. What was I supposed to say? *Hey, coach, the assistant
county prosecutor might be gunning for me so I've got to leave early?*
Yeah, she'd believe that.

Matt had texted me that the interview went well. The lady
pretty much told him the internship was his. Although I
wanted this opportunity for him, it complicated things.

He'd tried to convince me to hang out at his work. But now
that he'd interviewed, I couldn't continue hiding the truth.
He'd grown tired of waiting for me to tell him the name of my
abuser. I didn't blame him. A smart guy, Matt likely suspected
I had an important reason for withholding information.

The stress of *not telling* overwhelmed me. I didn't want to
see him until we had privacy.

So instead of spending time with him, I told him I didn't
need a freakin' babysitter. At this rate, he'd probably break up

with me *before* I told him.

Besides, I was fine. Now that I'd decided to confront my demons, or, more accurately, my *demon*, singular, I discovered a well of courage inside me, deeper than I'd ever imagined.

Plus, I had pepper spray. And it wasn't pink.

The lights of a passing car flashed in my window. A glance at the clock revealed I'd been sitting in my driveway for almost five minutes.

Screw it. I threw open the car door and stalked toward the house, vaguely registering the slamming of a car door down the street. Halfway to the brightly lit porch, a tingle of awareness ran up the back of my neck. I glanced around but saw nothing. I shoved the key at the keyhole, missed, and the keys dropped to the concrete.

I squatted to pick them up. My heart pounded. I tried to swallow my stupid fear. It was probably just another group of Girl Scouts lying in wait. Picturing the little girls in my mind, waiting to pounce with their Thin Mints and shortbread cookies, relaxed me a little. I inserted the key in the lock more carefully this time—

—and two hands slammed against the door on either side of my head. My heart jammed in my throat.

"You little bitch," a familiar voice hissed in my ear. The voice from my nightmares.

I didn't need to turn around to identify the intruder. The spicy scent of his cologne combined with the heat from his body to smother me.

I slipped a shaky hand into my pocket and fumbled with my phone, picturing the screen in my mind. Speed dial 1 was 911. Speed dial 2, Matt. Speed dial 3 through 9 and I was out of luck. I fumbled with the touch screen, hoping I'd called someone.

Warren removed his hands. Slowly, I turned to face him, shoving my shaking fingers into the pocket that held my spray. Once I had it in my grip, my pulse still raced, but unexpected confidence replaced fear.

Ever since the encounter in the restaurant, I'd prepared for the next time I ran into him. I refused to let him control my responses like he had before. I squared my shoulders and looked him right in the eye. "Well, if it isn't Warren Johnson. What brings you to Summit Heights?" That was for 911, just in case. Next, a little something for Warren. "Back off. You're in my space," I spat.

Not bad for someone whose heart had shifted into over-drive.

"I'm in your space? That's great." He glowered, keeping his voice low. "You turned me in for some bogus abuse claim." Then he smiled, the charming smile he used when chatting with his supporters.

But I saw right through the brightness to the endless depths of his black soul.

"Now, who's going to believe an overwrought, confused girl?" He eased back, adding inches between us. "Little beauty, you already recanted once," he whispered, just a breath of sound.

Air strangled in my throat. I thought I was prepared, but all it took was *little beauty* and I was eight years old. Alone, frightened, confused.

Helpless.

I forced myself to inhale and exhale, slow and steady, drawing courage with each breath. Staring into his eyes, I could see that he'd counted on my fear. He leaned toward me, and I smelled his spicy aftershave again. Only this time, that hated smell didn't make me weak. Nope. Now it pissed me off, and I clenched the spray more tightly. Suddenly I wasn't helpless or hopeless. I was powerful.

And he was an ass. A horrible, worthless man who preyed on little girls.

I wasn't a little girl anymore.

Stepping forward, I invaded *his* space. His smile faltered, and he stumbled back.

"Get off my property." I dared him to try and hurt me. Dared him with my eyes, my words, my posture. The cameras weren't installed yet, but I didn't care. I pulled the spray from my pocket and pointed it at him. No matter what happened to me, this asshole was going down.

It might not have been the smartest thing to do, but I tossed in, "Freaking pervert. Coward."

His face turned red as he started to lean in and then stopped when I raised the spray toward his face. The hatred in his eyes threatened to pierce my heart before it could jump out of my chest. I really, really hoped I was pointing the damn opening toward *him*.

"Hey, Mags!"

I'd never been so happy to hear that hated name. I enclosed the spray in my palm and allowed my arm to drop to my side.

"Sorry I'm late." Kelvin stomped up the steps, his eyes gleaming against the blackness of his face. He did that thing he does on the field where he appears bigger than he really is. He crowded his way onto the porch and stood by my side.

"Hey, man, remember me?" He stuck out his hand. "I'm Kelvin."

Warren slapped on his politician face. "Nice to see you again,

Kelvin."

They shook hands, and I bit back a smirk when Warren winced. I slipped the pepper spray back into my pocket.

"Oh, sorry man," Kelvin said, not at all sincere. He held tight to Warren's hand. "Football you know. Don't always know my own strength." He bestowed his own special smile on Warren, bright white and predatory. With a parting squeeze, he released the pervert's hand.

"Well, Maggie, tell your mom I stopped by to see how she's doing. Good to see you." Warren glared, the message unmistakable—*keep your damn mouth shut.*

Never, ever would I recant this time. Never.

He stalked the length of the driveway. Two houses down, he wrenched open the door of his Porsche and paused. Staring back at us, he waved all fake friendly, then hopped into the car, slammed the door and sped down the street.

Kelvin and I stood there in the glow of the porch light, watching as he disappeared from sight.

"What are you doing here?" I asked, then bit my lip. I'd spoken in my bitchy tone, a remnant from the encounter with Warren. "Sorry, I…"

"No problem. I happened to be in the neighborhood."

I stared at him, and then out of nowhere, I snorted.

"Did you…snort?" He raised his brow in an exaggerated attempt to put me at ease. Kelvin, the jerk, had a sweet side. Who knew?

I nodded, relief and a sense of power flowed through me. I'd made the call, faced the pervert and survived. Even if Kelvin hadn't shown up, I'd have sprayed Warren's lying face.

Still, I wondered what the heck Kelvin was doing here. Although, did I really need to ask? I'd never been so thankful

CHAPTER TWENTY-EIGHT

Matt insisted on watching out for me—even when I got mad at him for doing it.

I raised my brows right back at him. "So you were in the neighborhood? I'll bet you've never been on my street in your life."

"Says you." Kelvin of the snappy comeback.

"Says me." Two could play the lame game. "You want to come in for a soda?"

We eyed each other. We'd never been anything you could call friends. Hell, we'd barely been what I'd call civil.

Matt's truck cut a sharp turn into the driveway and jerked to a stop. He jumped out.

Kelvin glanced his way. "Nah, thanks. I'm supposed to be meeting some friends." He leaned in and gave me an awkward hug. "You're tough, girl."

He left, nodding to Matt as he leaped off the porch and cut through my front yard to head up the street.

Matt climbed the steps, his face pale. "You okay?"

"Yeah, I'm fine." I peered into the darkness. "Does Kelvin need a ride somewhere?"

"No. He parked on the next block."

"Did you send him to spy on me?"

"To make sure you were okay until I could get here." He surveyed the street. The tic in his jaw worked furiously. "If anything happened to you..."

When he turned to me, I glanced away, unable to meet his eyes. I didn't want this—I wasn't Matt's responsibility. I could handle myself. And if anything did happen to me, and Matt thought he was in charge of keeping me safe, it would destroy him.

And I couldn't live with that.

The silence between us grew. I didn't even need to look his way to know he watched me. The heat of his stare seared my flesh. Poor Matt, always waiting for me to finally take the next step.

Reluctantly, I faced him. His gaze captured mine. "You should have told me."

"What...?" The question died on my lips. I refused to insult us both by asking *what do you mean*. I already knew. He meant I should have told him it was Warren. Somehow, he'd found out. "How..."

He held up his phone.

I pulled my phone from my pocket. Speed dial 2.

Matt had heard everything.

Chapter Twenty-nine

*Once the truth was out, there was no shoving it back in
the box. Not this time.*
  —Maggie's Journal

You should have told me. Matt's accusation lingered between us.
It made me defensive.

"What did you tell Kelvin?" The best defense was a good
offense. Right?

Matt skewered me with that steady stare. I tapped my foot
against the ground. Okay, sure, I needed to explain about
Warren, but *he* needed to explain about Kelvin.

"He knows." My words held an edge of accusation. In all the
craziness, I hadn't even thought about what Matt might have
told Kelvin to get him here. He had no right to tell that jerk
anything!

Even though Kelvin might not be quite the jerk I'd labeled
him.

Matt sighed. "No, I told him the same story I told Ryan. That
you were having problems with your mom's old boyfriend."
He scanned the shadows before returning his gaze to me. "Shit,

I was right, wasn't I?"

I nodded.

"Why didn't you tell me?"

"I...I was waiting until after your interview." I turned up the corners of my mouth. "It went well?" I attempted cheery and supportive but fell short. Way short.

He ran his hand through his hair, disbelief plain on his face. "You can't think I'd actually work with that asshole?"

I could see the effort it took for him to remain calm. He was mad, and I wasn't sure how much anger was directed at Warren and how much was for me.

I wasn't afraid, but I was getting annoyed. Why was this hard for him to understand? I studied the tic in his jaw and chose my words carefully. "That's exactly why I didn't tell you. No matter what happens with me, this is a great opportunity for you."

He glowered. "Can we go inside?"

I grabbed my backpack from the porch, but when I tried to jab the key in the lock, my hand trembled, and I missed. I wasn't sure how much more I could handle tonight. And right now, Matt ranked high on the list of things stressing me out.

He cursed under his breath. Then, he put his hand over mine, and we unlocked the door together. I fought the urge to lean back against him and let go of the entire crappy day. He kissed the top of my head, but I'm pretty sure we both felt the tension that still pooled between us.

"Wait just a minute." He jogged back to his truck and pulled out his backpack and a bag from the local Chinese restaurant.

My eyes narrowed. "Why aren't you at work?"

He ushered me through the door. "Called in sick."

"What...you..."

He silenced me with a kiss. "I'm here, and you're stuck with me. Let's eat."

Our eyes locked as the outcome hung in the balance. With a not reluctant sigh, I caved. I wanted him here, and it was stupid to pretend otherwise. "I'm starving."

We didn't speak again until we'd made a dent in our meal of crab rangoon, moo shu pork, and chicken with pea pods. And my heart once again thudded along at normal speed.

Matt, of course, went first. "I understand why you didn't tell me. But…you don't have to protect me."

Ah, he understood. He just didn't agree. I raised my brow. "*You* don't have to protect *me*."

Stalemate. We each took another bite.

It was time for me to go first. "Look, I'm sure there are a lot of good people in the prosecutor's office. If Warren is arrested, you won't work for him. So, you needed to interview well." *If Warren was arrested…if.* My pulse started to race.

Matt growled deep in his throat. "If…it better not be *if.*" He looked away, the tic on his jaw beating so fast, I stared in fascination. Somehow, his struggle for control calmed me. *It better not be if.* We agreed on this point, and yet…sometimes life wasn't fair. Even if he overlooked that fact, I did not. Matt took a deep breath. The tic calmed, but I knew what he was thinking.

"You can't beat him up." I pointed my chopsticks at him. "Promise. You can't do anything."

Matt drummed his chopsticks against his plate.

"If you do something, it will make it worse. We need to see how this plays out."

The chopsticks stilled, and he nodded. "I won't do any-thing—as long as he keeps his distance. I find him threatening

161

you again, and he'll regret it."

I toyed with my food. That was good enough for now. I'd had enough drama for one night. I bit the inside of my lip and smiled. "Thank you for believing me."

"What does that mean?" His brow furrowed.

I hadn't expected a frown in return. "It means *thank you*?"

He shook his head. Not angry but confused. "Why wouldn't I believe you?"

"Uh, because he's your freakin' hero."

"Yeah, well not anymore. He's a creep. I should have seen it. I was too caught up in his fancy resume." He took another bite, chewed and swallowed, his forehead still creased with worry. "This will get ugly."

"I warned you." I observed him carefully. I didn't want him beating anyone up for me.

"You did."

Unexpectedly, I pictured my dad. It would have been okay if *he* beat up Warren. Of course, if he were alive there would have been no need. I fiddled with my chopsticks, frustrated that moisture gathered in my eyes.

Sometimes I was so tired of fighting alone.

"You need to stop keeping things from me. We need to be truthful with each other." Matt reached over and grabbed my hand, waiting for my response, willing me to agree.

This is why I didn't get close to people. Complete honesty scared me almost as much as reporting. But he was right. "I agree. We'll both be truthful. No hiding things."

He squeezed my hand. "I'm not leaving until your mom gets back."

I blinked. It would be awesome if he stayed.

It would be awesome not to be alone.

Then I considered his parents' reaction. "I'll be fine."

"Fine? You were up all night last night."

"How would you know?" For the first time, I noticed the dark circles under his eyes. "Matt?"

"I might have slept in my car. Out front." He shrugged. No big deal.

He'd watched over me all night. And I doubt he'd actually slept. Wow. At a loss for words, I glanced at my plate, my throat clogged with emotion. I hadn't been alone.

Then I started to worry again. "What about your parents?"

"They think I stayed with Ryan. Tonight, I already told them I wouldn't be home until your mom gets back. They're cool."

I stared at him for a long moment, reined in the mushy emotion, and called it like I saw it. "You're the best boyfriend I've ever had."

"Hmph." He acted like it was no big deal, but I could tell it pleased him. "I'm the only boyfriend you've ever had."

"Yeah, well, thanks for ruining me for any others."

We both smiled, and for a brief time, we were just a guy and a girl having dinner.

* * *

We studied for a couple of hours before kicking back and turning on the television. Matt stretched his arm over the sofa back and curled his hand around my shoulder. He kissed my head.

"I'm staying until your mom gets back."

I shrugged. *Fine by me.* I settled in against his chest.

"I'm glad you reported." His husky voice rang with conviction. "He's going to spend the rest of his miserable life in

163

jail."

I sighed, wanting to agree, but instead, delivered a large serving of reality. "It's not going to be that easy. He's Warren Johnson, for God's sake. Pillar of the community. Volunteer, entrepreneur, all around good guy."

And I'm the girl who recanted.

Matt cursed. "Except he's attracted to little girls."

I hated to argue the opposition's side, but he needed to understand. "Who's going to believe that? Maybe no one will believe me over him."

"Why are you so negative?" He pulled back to search my face.

I patted his shoulder, my ridiculously optimistic guy. "One of us has to keep it real. I just want you to be prepared."

"If you don't believe he'll get what's coming to him, why did you report?"

"I don't believe he won't, but I have to consider the possibility he might not get what he deserves." *And that I might not get what I deserve.* I shrugged. "And besides..." My voice trailed off.

His brow furrowed, and then his eyes lit with understanding. "The little girl at the restaurant."

I nodded.

He gathered me into his arms and held me tight for a long moment. When he pulled back, I read both tenderness and frustration on his face.

"At least that mom will be warned." Frustration underscored his words.

I told myself it would be enough if I could save another girl.

The way no one had saved me.

"It's not right," Matt concluded.

On this we both agreed.

Chapter Thirty

Jerry Garcia once said, "Somebody has to do something, and it's just incredibly pathetic that it has to be us." I know how he felt.

Except instead of pathetic, I find it annoying, infuriating and crazy making. It shouldn't be MY responsibility.

Should it?
  —Maggie's Journal

"Wake up," Matt whispered in my ear.

I stretched and cuddled closer. I'd found my happy place and didn't plan to leave.

Ever.

"Your mom's home."

Crap. I jerked upright, narrowly missing a collision with his jaw.

We sat up straight on the couch just as Mom entered from the garage. She stopped at the sight of us. Wrinkles creased her tailored navy suit. Storms brewed in her eyes.

"Oh, hello. It's nice to see you again, Matt," she greeted in monotone.

If she was glad to see him, she needed to tell her face. Nothing about her indicated welcome. A glance at Matt indicated an equal lack of *happy to see you*.

Leaving her travel bag near the door, she took a halting step forward.

"Hi, Mrs. Bryant." He kept his tone respectful if cool and looked from Mom to me.

"Thanks for waiting with me." My gaze flitted to Matt before fixing back on Mom.

Our gazes locked.

And held.

"It's, uh, pretty late." Matt interrupted our mother-daughter staring contest, a question lurking in his words.

I turned my back on Mom, my answer in my eyes. *You'd better leave.*

He grabbed his backpack, and I walked him to the door.

"You okay?" he mouthed.

I nodded. "Thanks."

He hesitated as if he wanted to kiss me…or stay. I took the decision away by planting a kiss on his lips, and then ushered him out.

I watched him all the way to his car. Once he'd pulled out of the driveway, I yanked the door shut, locked it, and faced the woman responsible for this whole mess.

Recant. Tell them you were confused.

Mom hadn't moved. Her energy swamped me, transforming the house from calm seas to roiling waters so quickly my head swam.

Her mouth opened and closed and opened again. "Warren

167

called me. He left a carefully worded message. 'I'm worried about Maggie. If you need help getting her into a counselor, let me know. I'm worried about her. And you.'"

She'd used air quotes around Warren's words. *Freaking air quotes.*

"Don't you understand?" She glared at me, her eyes brimming with overblown panic. "It was a warning."

Oh yeah? She had nothing on me. "Well, he stopped by to deliver a message to me in person."

That stopped her cold. She took a shuddering breath. "Are you okay?"

I'd like to say she cared, but her question smacked more of accusation. Or maybe I just couldn't see past my anger at *her*.

I nodded. "He came up behind me when I was trying to open the front door. Called me a bitch. Pretty much threatened me." I was proud of how calm my voice sounded.

Mom paced the room. "Oh my God," she muttered under her breath. "Oh my God. Oh my God." She stopped, stared at me, eyes glazed, and paced again, muttering all the while.

I knew it wasn't nice, but I itched to pepper spray her. Just a little urge. Nothing I'd ever act on.

I'd done the right thing. I didn't feel exactly good, but as good as you can feel in a crap situation like mine. I'd done the right thing—and she couldn't see the rightness of it. Even after all these years.

I wasn't naive enough—*stupid enough*—to believe anymore that Warren's perversions had been just about me.

This wasn't just about what I deserved.

It was about what the next little girl deserved. About what every little girl deserved. Someone to fight for her.

It hit me all at once. I had Matt to fight for me now. And in

168

a completely bizarre turn of events, Kelvin. Wasn't that what I wanted? Someone to care, to see the wrongness, to put me first?

I stared at my mom. No, I didn't want just anyone to protect me. I needed my mom to stand up for me. For once.

Mom stopped pacing.

"Maggie, honey. Please understand. I'm trying to protect you. He's a dangerous man. He'll hurt us." She stopped and considered her words. "He could hurt you. Physically. Emotionally. Socially. I know you think that doesn't matter, but you don't know. He's smart and connected and powerful. He'll destroy you. You have a good life, sweetie." She paused again. "What will your boyfriend think? What will everyone say when Warren goes on the attack? Maggie, it'll be bad. You have no idea."

Her words spewed out so quickly, starting and stopping, darting in one direction, then traveling down a different track. She made my head hurt.

And my heart. Why couldn't she support me?

"I'm sorry," I said. I meant to stop there, but the words tumbled out. "I'm sorry *you* don't understand me. That *you* can't support me." I heard my voice grow louder and louder, but couldn't find the off switch. "I'm sorry *you* don't see that this is the right thing to do. It's about me, yes. But it's also bigger than me." I threw my arms out wide. "It's about a little girl I saw with that asshole *you* brought into our lives."

By now I was screaming. Great. One of the neighbors would probably call the police. Whatever control I'd gained earlier was destroyed in round two with my mother.

I fled to the safety of my room.

Leaning against the door, I waited for my heart to stop

racing. I'd put something into motion that couldn't be stopped. Something I refused to stop. Only one barrier to justice remained.

What if no one besides Matt and Ms. Williams believed me?

* * *

The next morning, I sped toward the front door, leaving early, anxious to avoid any discussion with my mom. I whipped open the front door before her voice stopped me. Damn.

"Maggie."

I wanted to continue through the door, but at her pain-laced voice, I couldn't just storm out. But I didn't turn around either.

"I didn't listen to my messages until late last night. Children's Services is sending an investigator to talk with us at 4:00." She paused before continuing, her voice subdued. "Are you sure about this?"

I nodded.

"I'll call the school. Tell them you have a doctor's appointment. Be home by 4:00."

I nodded again and left the house before I smothered under her pain and fear.

Chapter Thirty-one

Sometimes I want to take it all back. The reporting. My challenging, walled-off, insecure life was easier.

Or maybe it's just the life I understood.
*   —Maggie's Journal*

I pulled into the driveway at 4:00. A blue sedan I didn't recognize pulled in behind me. Although logic told me it was the person from Children's Division, fight or flight response hissed, *"It's Warren."* Or one of his friends.

Or maybe he had his own thugs.

Prosecutors knew a lot of people—some of them criminals. My heart raced. I forced myself to step out of the car.

The driver's door opened, and a woman with curly red hair slipped out. She was neither slim nor fat. A couple of inches shorter than me, she wore a black jacket and pants, with a navy blue shell underneath. Her hazel eyes shown clear but weary with little lines stretching out from the corners. Her brown briefcase was scratched up, and her black shoes scuffed.

I noticed everything in mere seconds. Fight or flight had

definitely kicked in, causing my senses to open wide and overload on every detail. I took steading breaths, wiggled my toes in my shoes and willed my hyper-observant self to subside.

She smiled. It was a nice smile. I relaxed a little. I liked that she had red hair. Like my dad.

"Hello, I'm Beth Humerickhouse from Children's Services." Her voice had a musical quality. She shifted her briefcase and stuck out her hand.

"Hi, I'm Maggie Bryant." We shook, and for a moment, I just stared. This woman, with her tired, friendly smile and ugly suit was here for my story.

To listen.

And judge.

And help. *Please, please, to help.*

"Would you like to come in?" *Stupid, stupid.* Of course she wanted to come in.

"I would." She brushed her hair out of her face and followed me.

I opened the front door and discovered Mom standing in the family room, staring out into the backyard.

"Mom, this is Ms. Humerickhouse."

She turned to face us, her face devoid of color and emotion.

"Hello, Mrs. Bryant. It's good to meet you." She shook Mom's hand. "Please, both of you, call me Beth."

Mom and I sat on opposite ends of the couch. Beth sat in the chair across from us. She tucked a curl behind her ear and perched reading glasses on her nose.

"Today, I'm going to ask some basic questions. A more detailed interview will be conducted by a forensic investigator."

She paused, so I nodded.

"I'd like to talk with each of you separately, if that's okay."
This time Mom and I both nodded.

"Why don't I start with Maggie." Beth looked at my mom.

"I'll go in the kitchen and start dinner," Mom said as she stood and disappeared, ghost-like, into the other room.

Once again, I told my story. Really not much more detail than when I called the hotline.

It was different, though, telling a real person...a stranger. Was it my fault if my voice sounded like broken glass when I finished? "My mom told me to recant."

"Thank you, Maggie." Beth's smile warmed me, and yet...that was it?

Didn't she believe me? My fingers tapped rapidly against my knee. Surely we weren't finished.

She reached above her glasses to squeeze the bridge of her nose. "Would you get your mom? You and I will talk again before I leave, but I need to talk with her privately now."

Both relieved and worried that we weren't finished, I hurried into the kitchen. "Mom."

She jumped, her hand to her chest. "Maggie! You scared me to death."

There was no evidence of dinner in sight. "She's ready for you." I grabbed my backpack and stalked to my room without another word.

I plopped down on the bed and pulled out my Calculus book, opened it to the assignment and...

...did nothing.

I checked my phone. Nothing from Matt. Of course not. He was still at football.

Jumping off the bed, I paced my room. *What was Mom saying?* With a heavy sigh, I crossed to my door and opened it very quietly, very slowly, a very tiny amount.

One benefit of a small house—it was easy to eavesdrop. If I hadn't been so emotionally churned up, I would never have fully shut the door in the first place.

Beth's voice drifted down the hall. "You told Maggie to recant?" She asked, neutral, as if she'd asked what we had for breakfast.

That ticked me off. I wanted accusation and judgment.

"You told Maggie to recant?" She demanded a response, her disdain apparent. Something more like that.

I cracked the door open wider and peeked around the frame in time to see Mom nod, the movement brittle, jerky. "I did ask her to recant." I could see her face and the back of Beth's curly head.

"You said you didn't know he was abusing her. Did you believe her?"

"No. I mean, yes, I mean I didn't know. After she told Mari...I...I could see how it was true." She tilted her head back and closed her eyes. "I didn't want to believe it. But..." Her voice faded away. She blinked and lifted her head, squaring her shoulders, hands clasped in her lap. "He gave her so much...toys, clothes, candy, that pink princess bedroom. He read to her, rubbed her back. Still she would ask not to be left with him."

Mom swiped at her eyes. "It never occurred to me. But it should have. And maybe I knew *something* was wrong, but I... after she told, yes, I believed her."

"Why did you tell her to recant?" Ms. Humerickhouse leaned forward.

I couldn't see her face, but the weary posture was gone. She teemed with intensity.

Mom's eyes narrowed. "You know who he is. He's powerful. He knows people. Bad people."

She glanced down the hall, right at me, and I ducked back into my room, hoping she hadn't noticed.

"He promised it wouldn't happen again." Silence. "Maggie," she called, her voice sharp.

Busted. I stepped into the hall.

"It didn't happen again, right?"

I nodded, walking back to join them. "Right." It angered me, the way she said this. As though that made what she did okay. "But I could feel him watching me." Our eyes locked, another skirmish in our battle of wills. A battle in which there was never a winner.

"Are you saying he admitted to abusing Maggie?" Beth interrupted our staring contest.

Mom jerked her gaze back to the social worker. "No. He said he'd make sure nothing would happen again that might cause confusion."

Confusion. Frustration roiled inside me, my hand clenching into a tight fist. Finger by finger, I forced myself to relax.

"You moved out of his house, correct?" Beth continued.

A little too matter of fact for me.

Mom sat very still. "Yes."

Beth reviewed her notes, tapping the pencil against her mouth. "Two months after Maggie recanted." A frown creased her brow as she turned her attention back to Mom. "You bought a house after you moved out? Didn't you say you'd been renting before?"

Mom glanced at me out of the corner of her eye and wrapped a lock of her hair around her finger. "He gave me money to help with the house."

Electricity crackled in the air. My anger generated a lot of heat.

"He gave you money." Beth nibbled on the end of her pencil. "Did he pay you to convince her to recant?"

Bile churned in my stomach, rose in my throat. She took money from that bastard. Traded money for her silence.

Mom shook her head vehemently. "No! No, I wouldn't do that. He threatened us. He did. Later, he said he was sorry, and he offered me money. I took it." She turned to me. "For us. For you. So we could live in this house in a nice neighborhood and you could go to a good school. He owed us."

I shook my head.

"He owed *you*," she insisted.

I clenched both hands, needing time to absorb my mom's choices.

"Mrs. Bryant," Beth spoke sharply. "You said he apologized? Apologized for…"

My eyes widened. I hadn't even considered this. He'd admitted abusing me? And still…

"No," Mom shook her head. "He was very careful with his words. He just said he was sorry things didn't work out. But I knew what he meant."

"Okay, thank you. Maggie, would you give me a tour of the house?"

"Uh, yeah, sure." Anything to get away.

We walked through the house. Beth made notes in her three-ring-binder as we passed each room. We paused in my bedroom. She checked the window locks. "Does your mom have men over?" she asked.

"Not really. Usually they go out or to his place. She's dating a guy named Marvin. Seems nice. No pervert vibes."

CHAPTER THIRTY-ONE

"I know this isn't easy." She checked the lock on my bedroom door.

"No, it's not. I'm okay, though."

"Do you feel safe?"

I hesitated, then nodded. I felt as safe here as I would anywhere, I guessed.

Biting the inside of her lip, she slipped her glasses off her nose and into her pocket. She rubbed the bridge of her nose wearily. "Okay then."

We returned to the family room.

"Mrs. Bryant, Maggie, thank you for meeting with me."

What? This was it? She'd barely asked me anything. Not about the actual abuse. Not that I looked forward to giving her the horrid details, but this...?

"Although Maggie is not in danger of sexual abuse now, due to Warren Johnson's powerful position in the community I'm going to walk this report into the police station. We'll set a meeting with the forensic investigator right away, and then the police will want to talk with you."

Relief that she believed me flooded in, only to be washed away by a tide of fear.

She smiled at me. "Maggie, the investigator will gather more details from you. I'm just here to make sure you are in a safe home environment and confirm credible suspicion of abuse. I'll recommend speedy follow up despite the fact that you are in a safe environment. Warren's power in this community is an extenuating circumstance."

She reached in her binder and handed each of us her card. "You call if you need anything. Make sure you let us know if he tries to contact you."

I tucked the card in my jeans pocket. We'd failed to mention that one thing. I cleared my throat. "He came here."

"Here? Warren? He came to this house?"

Nodding, I clarified. "Last night. He was waiting for me." I explained what had happened. "And he called my mom."

Worry creased Beth's brow. "We should find another place for y—"

"No." The word escaped more sharply than I'd intended. "I'm fine. My mom's here." I sensed Mom's surprise. "And when she's not, my boyfriend can stay here." Despite the seriousness of the conversation, my heart did a little flip at calling Matt *my boyfriend* for the first time.

Reluctance written on her face, she conceded. "Maggie, you shouldn't be alone at any time. Ms. Bryant, if you're not with Maggie, make sure she's with someone you trust." She grasped her briefcase as if it armed her for battle, tapping her finger against her chin with her free hand. "Excuse me. I'll be right back." She stepped outside onto the front porch.

I spied from the window as she pulled her phone from her pocket and hit speed dial. With her body angled toward the street, she spoke into the phone, making it impossible for me to read her lips. Not that I'd ever been any good at lip-reading. She hung up and fished her binder out of her briefcase to make more notes. Vaguely, I registered the sound of Mom banging pots and pans in the kitchen.

Beth's phone must have rung, because she answered it. This time she turned toward the house, and our eyes met. The hard look on her face softened. She smiled, reassuring with an edge of teeth. Twisting a loose piece of hair around my finger, I nodded, continuing to stare until she turned away.

A moment later, a police car pulled into our driveway.

Twenty minutes after that, I had another business card, and

178

Warren had a restraining order headed his way—although it would take a couple of days before he was served.

"The forensic investigator will contact you tomorrow." Beth shook hands first with Mom and then with me. "Then the detectives will talk with you. If you're afraid, call 911. Even if you're not positive you're in danger."

The magnitude of what I was doing settled on my shoulders once again, weighing me down. Part of me longed for the days when night terrors and dating choices were my biggest concern.

"Do you have any questions for me?"

Now that the investigation was moving forward, I had only one question.

When would this all be over?

I feared I already knew the answer.

Never.

Chapter Thirty-two

.

The great wheel of ugly truth has been put into motion, threatening everyone in its path. I pray each day that it crushes Warren and spares everyone else.

I don't know much about prayer. I hope I'm doing it right.
  —Maggie's Journal

Beth had called less than an hour after leaving our home to schedule an appointment for the next morning, Saturday, at the Child Protection Center.

I texted Matt, canceling our breakfast plans, and my glass-is-half-full-guy replied, "Ok. Will install cameras while gone."

I stuck my key under the doormat so they could get inside if they needed to. Not the safest place for keys, but Matt and Ryan planned to pull up right after we left.

Mom and I hopped in the car.

Together.

Just how I wanted to spend my weekend. Instead of starting Saturday by hanging with Matt, I was spending the morning with my mom, heading to the Child Protective Center, and talking with a forensic investigator about my abuse.

In detail.

My morning pretty much sucked.

Someone called a Family Advocate met us in the reception area and accompanied me during the forensic interview. This was the detailed description of what had happened.

When did it happen? Where? What was I wearing? What was Warren wearing? Where was Mom? Describe the room, the sheets on the bed, the abuse. The questions were never-ending. But when the interview finished, I'd shared everything.

Although I tried to remain distanced and unemotional—again like a reporter sharing the facts—the interview drained me.

I declined my mom's invitation to lunch, having had enough of both her and the topic of abuse. Relieved we had Saturday volleyball practice and anxious to flee, I insisted on going to school. At volleyball, I understood the rules and what it took to win.

* * *

After practice let out, I took my time in the locker room. By the time I exited, everyone else had left. Even the hall loomed, silent and empty. Leaning against the wall, I scrolled through my social media feed. Casual, as if checking to see what my friends were up to.

Nothing important.

Then the local news alert popped up. I'd set it that morning.

Breaking News: Local prosecutor accused of child sexual abuse.

Ohmygod. My legs gave out, and I slumped onto the concrete floor. The wheels of justice, absent for most of my life, now rolled unerringly toward me.

Assuring myself I would not be crushed beneath their weight, I tapped the link.

Warren Johnson, assistant county prosecutor, has been accused of molesting an eight-year-old girl. The alleged victim, currently seventeen-years-old, reported Johnson to the child abuse hotline. Sources close to the investigation stated they were investigating the facts.

Johnson is believed to be the frontrunner in the race for County Prosecutor. He graduated from Lakeview High School. A highly sought after football recruit, Johnson played for Notre Dame before attending Harvard Law School. He is active in a number of local charities and a recipient of the coveted Governor's Service Award.

This was unbiased reporting? They made him sound like a freakin' saint. I squeezed my eyes shut and forced deep, calming breaths.

Mr. Johnson's charitable foundation issued the following statement: We have no comment regarding the accusations. Warren has been a respected leader and philanthropist in this community for nearly a decade.

I stared at the feed. Two comments. Five comments. Seven—I tried to ignore them, tried to get off the bench and go home.

I tried.

But instead I tapped *Comments.*

I always thought he was creepy.

I exhaled. I wasn't the only one. I kept reading.

He's a great guy. Helped my family put away the monster that killed my mom. No way he did this.

Our prayers are not only for Warren and his family, but also for the unfortunate young lady who, regardless of the true facts, needs our compassion and understanding at this time.

He's lying. No way can nobody trust lawyers. They lie.

He's one of the nicest guys I know. He's always helping at the food pantry. I don't believe this.

Some stupid slut wants attention.

I'd been painted as a confused girl to be pitied or a slut. Great. I'd pass on both. I bit my lip with enough force that I tasted blood. One of the two comments supporting me was no more than the rant of a nutcase.

Seven comments. Five for Warren, two against. And this was only the beginning.

The news app alerted me to three new comments. My hand hovered, shaking. I didn't want to know, and yet...

"Maggie?" Matt's concerned voice interrupted my internal debate.

I raised my eyes to his. "Hey." My voice trembled. *Damn it.*

His hand closed over mine and slipped the phone from my grasp. He dropped it in his jacket pocket. My eyes narrowed. He must have seen the article—and the comments.

"They don't know anything." He grabbed my hand and tugged me up so I tumbled against his chest. He gave me a quick squeeze and grabbed my backpack before I could speak. "Let's get dinner. I'm starving."

Who did he think he was? I snatched my backpack away from him. We stared at each other for a long moment. I read nothing but caring and concern in his eyes.

I shrugged. *Whatever.* I was hungry anyway.

My phone remained in his pocket.

For now.

Chapter Thirty-three

"We're all broken. That's how the light gets in." (I'm not sure who said this, but I like it.)
   —Maggie's Journal

Monday morning, Matt texted me that he had to meet the football coach before school, so I headed to my first class alone—and nervous.

I felt people's eyes on me as I traveled down the hall. Was I imagining it? Sure, I was a little paranoid. But I knew that feeling of being watched. I made eye contact with the girl who sat next to me in second hour and smiled. She looked away.

Conversations paused when I walked by.

My heart dropped to my stomach. I wasn't paranoid. I was the center of everyone's attention. My great fear had come true.

They knew. That was the only explanation.

Somehow, everybody knew.

Even though minor's names are supposed to be kept out of the news, they'd found out I'd reported Warren. I kept my chin up and walked faster, eyes focused on my classroom at the end of the hall. Half way there, someone slammed into my shoulder. My books fell to the floor. I spun around and nearly flattened Warren's nephew, the annoying Wyatt.

"Bitch," he jeered.

He knew.

"Back off," I shot back. I straightened my shoulders, but it took everything I had not to turn and run. I'd suspected he'd be trouble, but I hadn't thought it would happen this soon or this publicly. *Warren, Jr.* Big smile with too-white teeth, sketchy green eyes—an all-around arrogant ass.

I stood my ground and said nothing, my books splayed on the floor around us. I refused to crouch down in front of him and pick them up.

The buzz of voices grew hushed and louder all at the same time.

"You and your slut mom never got over my uncle dumping you. So now you try to get even by accusing him of sexual abuse."

He emphasized the word sexual as if somehow the accusation tainted me and not his damned uncle. *Idiot.*

He wasn't finished yet. "As if people like the Johnsons would ever be interested in trash like you." His voice carried throughout the hall.

If my peers hadn't known before, they knew now. I surveyed the surrounding faces—appalled, curious, dismayed, pity-filled, and obnoxiously nosy.

Damn, damn, damn. I refocused on Wyatt, who regarded me with disdain. Completely inappropriate laughter threatened to emerge.

I sobered as it hit me. He was blaming me for abuse that occurred *when I was eight years old.*

Asshole.

I bit the inside of my lip to keep from shrieking that no decent person would ever be interested in an eight-year-old. The last thing I wanted was an even bigger scene.

He edged closer, attempting to tower over me, except it didn't exactly work. I was almost as tall as he was.

"Your mom put you up to this?" He waved his arms. "You already tried to pull this shit once. Then changed your story."

Blood drained from my face. How did he know that? My mom's words rushed back. *You have no idea how this could destroy us.*

"Yeah, that's right," he ranted. "I heard you pulled this once before and then changed your mind. You trying to get money out of him again or what?"

The money. Wyatt knew everything—or a twisted version of the truth. My resolve waivered. Eyes stared. Voices whispered, then fell silent. Everywhere people stared at me, judging me.

What had I done?

The hall grew so quiet that I heard the sound of each person's breathing.

I, who had worked so hard in high school to stay under the radar, now stood front and center in a drama I'd never wanted. A drama I didn't deserve.

A drama in which I had no choice.

It'll be bad. You have no idea. My mother's words haunted me. And as much as I hated to admit it, she was right.

Damn her.

Broad shoulders shoved between Wyatt and me.

Kelvin.

"Back out of the lady's personal space. Don't you pay attention in class? Respect p-e-r-s-o-n-a-l space." He drew the

186

word out, pushing outward and to the side with outstretched hands. Kelvin parting the sea.

Wyatt stepped back to avoid contact. His frown deepened.

Clenching my hands to hide my trembling, I decided grabbing my books and getting out of here was better than standing my ground. I started to squat and pick them up, but Kelvin grabbed my arm and kept me upright.

"You make my friend here drop her books?" His question rang with accusation.

This guy knew how to tower over someone. Relief flooded through me. Someone had my back.

"She's clumsy." Wyatt blustered, but he took another step back.

"Pick 'em up." Not a request. More of a threat.

Wyatt hesitated, indecision stamped on his face. Lose face and pick up the books or refuse and possibly encounter a large, powerful, angry Kelvin when no one was around to save him.

He scanned the waiting faces. I read calculation in his eyes.

"She's a slut like her mother," he sneered.

Kelvin tensed beside me. I grabbed his arm. I did not want a fight.

A fist flew past my left ear, catching Wyatt square in the jaw. He stumbled back and would have fallen except Matt dove after him, grabbing his shirtfront and jerking him upright. Blood trickled down the side of Wyatt's mouth.

Damn it!

Matt drew his fist back for a second punch, and Kelvin and I lunged at the same time, pulling him away. Wyatt lurched forward with a wild swing that clipped Matt's jaw. The momentum from his swing carried him forward as he lost his balance and stumbled to the floor.

187

"Oops, watch it," Kelvin muttered.

I'm pretty sure Wyatt sprawled on the floor courtesy of Kelvin's well placed foot. Oops, indeed. He tripped the guy. *Nice.*

"Sorry I'm late. Are you okay?" Matt's harsh voice, so unlike him, drew me back to the nightmare of the moment. He grasped my hand, the tic in his jaw fluttering wildly. All around us people whispered and stared.

If he wanted to have my back, he'd missed the mark. This kind of support I definitely didn't need.

I jerked my hand from his. "What the hell were you thinking?"

He brows came together in a deep V. "I…"

"What's going on here?" Ms. Williams called. The crowd parted to let her through.

Just when I'd thought the situation couldn't get worse.

Wyatt moaned on the floor, playing his non-injury for all it was worth. Oh sure, he had a red mark on his chin where Matt punched him, but it would hardly leave a bruise.

What had Matt been thinking?

"Matt went berserk for no reason and punched me." Wyatt struggled to a sitting position. He probed his jaw, moaning slightly.

"Oh for God's sake, get off the floor. You're embarrassing yourself," Kelvin scoffed. He turned to our teacher. "They both took a swing. Wyatt here just couldn't swing and keep his balance. Everyone's fine, Ms. Williams."

Kelvin? I'd never heard such respect or educated enunciation from him. *Ever.*

While I remained frozen in place, Matt crouched down and gathered my books.

CHAPTER THIRTY-THREE

I glared at his back. He'd made everything worse.

Ms. Williams scanned the guilty parties—from Wyatt to Matt to Kelvin. Finally, her gaze landed on me. Understanding shone in her eyes. She sighed. "Matt and Wyatt, with me. Everyone else, get to class." She waved students away. "Go on. The show's over."

Our audience broke up. Ms. Williams headed down the hall with Wyatt.

Matt hung back. "Maggie, listen, I'm sorry." He held my books in one arm and reached for my face with his free hand.

The spell that held me silent shattered. "Get away from me," I hissed, shoving my palms against his chest.

Emotionless, he handed me my books and stepped back.

"Matt," Ms. Williams summoned him.

He hesitated a moment longer. "I'll see you later." When I remained silent, he bestowed a crooked smile, turned, and jogged after Ms. Williams and Asshole Junior.

"Don't bother." I called to his retreating form.

He didn't answer.

Kelvin tapped my arm. I whirled around and stepped back at the same time.

"Give him a break. He cares about you. He's had a tough morning."

"*He cares about you,*" I mocked. "What's the matter with you? I liked you better when you were a jerk."

To my surprise, he smiled. "Now you've hurt my feelings. When you thought I was a jerk you didn't like me at all." Squaring his shoulders, he puffed up, a frown marked his dark forehead. He deepened his voice. "I'm still a jerk."

"Yes, you are," I agreed, but my accusation lacked any real heat. I'd seen his nice side, and there was no going back.

189

He shrugged. "I'm just saying he did what needed doing. Give the guy a break. He stood up for you."

I gritted my teeth, forcing back a rude retort.

"He was upset."

My eyes narrowed. Matt hadn't acted like Matt. Kelvin wasn't acting like Kelvin. "What aren't you telling me?"

The bell rang. Neither of us moved.

"He was already hot. The coach accused you of making it up. Tried to convince Matt to talk to you. Warren's a big supporter of the football program." He rubbed his forefinger and thumb together, indicating money. Then, he shrugged, but his eyes sparked with anger. "Matt's off the team."

"The coach kicked him off?" Like that, my humiliation faded away, replaced by red hot fury. "He can't do that."

Kelvin stared at me, his normal, cocky self gone. Sadness marked his expression. Then, he shook his head. "No. Matt quit."

He quit? The cloak of silence enveloped me again, keeping me quiet even as Ms. Williams reappeared and handed us both passes so we wouldn't be tardy for class. As if that mattered.

I'd never asked for this. I was furious. At Matt.

At myself.

I should never have drawn him into this mess.

Sure, he'd been stupid, but more importantly, he'd *changed*. The calm, reasonable guy I'd fallen for had lost his temper and started a fight at school.

He'd quit the football team with no regard for his college future.

Once he'd had it all together, but not anymore. I'd broken him.

And I couldn't forgive him for that.

* * *

School dragged on like a bad movie. People whispering, then shutting up when I looked their way. Silence when I entered a classroom. Pitying glances from teachers.

I walked to my seat in each class, eyes straight ahead, asking for nothing more than anonymity. Something that now rested forever beyond my reach. Despair swamped me, leaving me brittle inside, but I refused to disintegrate in a useless heap on the floor.

Ms. Williams stopped me between classes. Asked if I needed anything. If I wanted to talk to the counselor. I told her no. I was fine.

Matt wasn't in seventh hour. I didn't see him after school.

My teammates were mostly nice, a couple even hugged me, but they didn't really know me. Although based on the hushed conversations that ceased when I arrived at practice, they all knew *about* me.

Mari wasn't there. She was on a college visit. Maybe that was for the best.

Somehow I went through the motions at practice and then jogged to my car afterward, although, really, I had nowhere to go. Home meant Mom and *that* nightmare.

I'd dumped Matt for losing his cool, because God knows I never lost control. *Stupid.*

I could call Kelvin. How weird was that? But his loyalty belonged to Matt.

After a brief moment of blessed belonging, I'd managed to cut myself off from anyone who mattered—or cared.

Chapter Thirty-four

Some parts of the journey, a girl makes alone.
  —Maggie's Journal

My phone vibrated as I put my car into reverse. Not Matt. Not that I expected him to call—or wanted him to.

I didn't recognize the number and let it go to voicemail. Shoving the car back into park, I laid my head back against the seat and closed my eyes.

The last forty-eight hours had taken a toll.

The phone vibrated in my hand, alerting me that I had voicemail. I tapped play.

"This is Detective Tori Dunning of the Lake Pleasant Police Department calling for Maggie Bryant. Maggie, we'd like for you to come to our headquarters at 10th and Main to talk. I'll be here until six tonight or you can call me at…" Her message continued, but the words failed to register.

Beth was right. They'd moved fast.

Since I didn't have plans and didn't want to go home, why not get this over with tonight? Reluctantly, I called my mom, but she didn't pick up. After leaving a brief message that she could meet me at the station if she wanted to—I didn't *need* her there—I turned my radio up full blast and headed for the LPPD.

The closer I got, the harder my heart beat. I pulled the CRV into a visitor parking spot, turned off the ignition, and stared at the three-story red building as I listened to the message in its entirety. Second floor. Detective Dunning.

Fight or flight.

It made me angry that I felt threatened. *I am the victim,* I told the stern, unwelcoming brick. Then, I hopped out of the car, slammed my door, and stalked across the pavement. I hesitated. *I am a survivor,* I told myself.

I climbed the five steps to the massive glass front doors. *Lake Pleasant Police Department.* I puffed up my cheeks and huffed out a breath.

The dominoes were falling, and I had no idea when they would stop—or where. Even though I'd been the one to topple the first domino, the chain reaction continued, out of my control. Horrible though it was, I wouldn't change it—I'd had no choice from the moment Warren called Ashley's name. Ashley who'd opened her little hands to show me the broken moth, her too-knowing eyes pleading for help.

Following the directions from the voicemail, I took the elevator to the second floor and approached the reception desk. Reception desk? There were no mints or toothpicks. Just a scratched wooden desk and an unsmiling middle-aged woman.

"I'm here to see Detective Dunning."

"Name?"

Nice to see you, too. "Maggie Bryant."

"Have a seat." She pointed with her pen to a series of five

brown padded chairs that faced a set of double doors.

I hated waiting. It meant the domino stopped and swayed in mid-air, and I didn't know when, or if, it would knock the next domino down.

I wanted everything to go away, but since that wasn't going to happen, I wanted things to move quickly, leaving me no time to think…or worry. I sat and pulled out my phone.

Then stuck it back in my pocket. There'd be no messages from Matt. I had no desire to see any more headlines on social media. I…

The right door swung open. "Maggie."

A short, powerfully built woman addressed me. She wore a pair of navy pants and a khaki jacket. Her blond hair hung in a neat ponytail at her nape, her only makeup a little blush and mascara. Her piercing blue eyes looked not at me, but into me, and yet I felt welcomed. I liked how she appeared both kind and bad ass all at the same time. That's a look I wanted to perfect.

"Thanks for coming down." She stuck out her hand. "I'm Detective Tori Dunning."

I stood and met her half way. We shook hands. "Let's go inside. I have a conference room where we can talk privately." We passed through the double doors and entered a world of desks and phones and controlled chaos. "We can wait for your mom in here." She waved toward an open door.

I shook my head. "She's not coming."

Detective Dunning knit her brow. "Your mom's already here. We interviewed her while you were at practice."

I stared at a point beyond her shoulder. Mom was here? I should have been relieved, but doubt consumed me. Had she undermined my claim? Painted me as a liar?

Recant.

"Maggie? We asked your mom to come early so we could talk with her separately. It's standard."

She escorted me to a little conference room. Not the kind you see on television where you can be handcuffed to the table or floor, thank God. But just a regular room with a table and six not-comfortable chairs. She shut the door behind us.

"Would you like something to drink?"

"No, thank you."

"We realize the courage it took for you to come forward. I'm going to ask you..."

Another woman entered, reviewing the contents of a file. She greeted me with a smile, her chin length auburn hair tucked behind her ear. "Hi Maggie, I'm assistant county prosecutor Sarah McKnight."

"Ms. McKnight." I shook her hand, offering a weak smile in return.

"Call me Sarah."

My mom entered behind her, and my smile fell. Mom's worried eyes sought mine. I could see she'd been crying. *Great.*

The four of us sat, Mom and me on one side. Detective Dunning and Prosecutor Sarah McKnight on the other.

Detective Dunning kicked it off. "Maggie, before we start, I want you to know your mom has already expressed her concern that Warren will find a way to hurt you or her. It is very unusual for a person accused of child sexual assault to retaliate. They're too busy trying to appear innocent, and retaliation ruins that."

I nodded.

"However, we understand Warren already approached you at your house.

Huh, if approached was a synonym for threatened.

She continued as if I'd spoken aloud. "The restraining order will be issued to Warren this evening. If he comes near you again, call 911. He doesn't have to threaten you for you to call—he's not allowed within 100 yards."

The length of a football field. I'd prefer 100 miles, but this sounded good. They were taking my report seriously. A tiny bit of tension leached from my shoulders.

"That's not enough," Mom protested. Her hands trembled. "Everyone likes him, you can't just…"

I glared at her. Even I knew there wasn't much more that could be done.

"We're going to give you the name of a community organization that can help with installing a security system if—"

"You don't get it. Everyone thinks he's a great guy. He can—"

"Mom," I interrupted. "There are already cameras installed." I told them about my birthday present from Matt.

Matt.

Detective Dunning nodded. "That's good." She slid a card toward us. "This group will help you with the cost of monitoring if you need it." She stared at my mom a moment before reaching across the table to touch her hand. "This isn't about anyone liking or not liking Warren Johnson. My job is to find the truth. If the truth is he's guilty, we'll do whatever we can to file charges that stick."

That got my attention. A chill ran down the back of my neck. "And if you decide he's not guilty?"

Detective Dunning and Sarah McKnight exchanged glances. Sarah leaned forward, studying me intently. "We are taking this investigation very seriously. I can't say more now, but you should know we believe you."

They believed me. *Thank God, thank God, thank God.* I sagged a little in my chair as relief crept into my bones.

With their support to sustain me, once again, I answered questions.

I told them everything. How I'd blocked the abuse until I was fourteen. The truths uncovered in my sessions with Doc Shirk. How he'd groomed me, starting with saving me from my fear of the dark, comforting me and rubbing my back, sneaking me candy. Asking *do you like this? Does it feel good?* Twisting things around so that my little girl mind thought the things I hated were really my fault.

The specifics of the abuse. How and where he touched me.

That he was careful never to do anything that would leave evidence of his actions.

Second grade and telling Mari the truth.

Warren's surprise visit. Matt and Kelvin having my back.

The meeting with Children's Division.

My mom telling me I had to say I was confused. Telling me I had to recant.

Mom sniffled. All color had drained from her face. She clutched a tissue in her hands, but I gave her credit. She didn't actually bawl this time.

Five o'clock passed. Then six. Seven.

Finally, the interview ended. I was more than a little tired of telling my story. Only this time instead of exhaustion, I felt...empty...numb. I'd poured everything out and only a cavernous emptiness remained.

I missed Matt.

We all headed for the door, but Sarah hesitated with her hand on the knob. "Your identity is supposed to be kept confidential because you're a minor. But if this case goes to trial..."

I'd be eighteen. Legally an adult. Media wouldn't be as careful. Well, it really didn't matter. "Everybody knows."

Sarah frowned.

"Warren's nephew goes to our school. He told everyone."

My mom gasped, a tiny intake of breath, but I heard it.

I turned to her. "You warned me." Shrugging, I ignored her concerned expression and stared at the women I was counting on. "He already got the football coach to pressure my boyfriend into getting me to recant." Amazing how quickly *boyfriend* fell from my lips despite my earlier outburst. "It didn't work."

Detective Dunning rewarded me with a smile. "Good for you. Anything like this, we want to know about it. Right away. The restraining order—"

"Will be delivered tonight," the prosecutor interrupted.

She and Tori exchanged glances, leaving me wondering if they were hiding something. I let it go. Honestly, I was too drained to care.

"We're going to move quickly," Sarah added. "You've both been very helpful."

"Maggie." My mom searched my face. "I am helping. I know you think about me as...as the bad guy, but I was just trying to keep you safe. It wasn't all about me."

This was why we'd never see eye to eye. Her idea of keeping me safe varied greatly from mine.

But maybe we'd strike some kind of compromise. A kind of uneasy peace that was better than what we'd had for the past few years. I'd forced her into it, but she *was* helping.

"What about Ashley?" The little girl with her purple dress and rhinestone kitty shirt weighed on my mind.

"Children's Division has already talked with her mom. That's all I can tell you for now."

My mom ran nervous fingers through her hair. I hoped Ashley's mom went straight into battle for her—unlike mine.

Chapter Thirty-five

The idea of being normal fascinates me. What do normal people think about each day? What do they do? How do they feel?

Doc says normal is a myth, a fantasy. It doesn't exist, and if it did, it would be boring.

Still...I'd like to know.
  —Maggie's Journal

As Detective Dunning escorted us down the hall, a familiar voice, angry and loud, startled me.

"Get these cuffs off me. I have rights, and I'm gonna sue your ass."

Kelvin?

Kelvin!

He stood in front of the booking desk, hands cuffed behind him.

No! My fault. Warren had struck against another person on the short list of people I cared about.

The officer with him appeared unimpressed. "Yeah, well, next time you'll think twice before threatening a man like Warren Johnson. He's a *prosecutor*, you know."

I started forward, my voice raised. "He did not—"

"Not now." Mom's panicked whisper stopped me.

My eyes fastened on Kelvin in horror. My mind searched for a solution. What should I do? How could I make things better, not worse?

Kelvin winked.

What? This was not the time for his cocky crap.

"Let's get this over with." Warren strode into view, his back to us. "I need to get home to dinner. My fiancé and our little...girl are waiting for me."

My heart jumped into my throat. Warren's voice filled the busy room—the voice of authority. Of course, this was no coincidence. The bastard had known I was here.

Maybe I was stupid, but that pause in the middle of *little...girl*? He'd done that on purpose, knowing, *knowing*, how my heart would race in anticipation of the hated *little beauty*.

He'd done it on purpose. Or maybe I was being stupid.

Maybe I was going crazy.

Someone laid a hand on my arm. I jerked sideways before I realized it was Sarah. "Relax," she murmured. "This is good. Trust me."

Good? *Good!?* "That's Kelvin," I insisted. She didn't realize what was happening.

"Patience. He'll be okay."

Detective Dunning left our little group and joined Warren. "Warren, what brings you here this late in the evening?"

"Tori, good evening. Just helping straighten out some of our city's youth."

201

"What happened?" she asked, her voice friendly.

"This unfortunate young man accosted me, threatened me when I stopped by the home of a friend to check on her daughter."

I'd had enough. As if the sight of my friend in handcuffs weren't enough, now Warren was twisting everything. I ignored Sarah's advice and lunged forward. "He did not accost you. He protected me. He heard you threaten me."

Warren whirled to face me, exaggerated surprise stamped on his face. "Maggie, my dear, what are you doing here?" He frowned. "This boy's influence over you is stronger than we feared. Thank God your mom asked me to check on you."

"Tina called you?" Detective Dunning crossed her arms and tilted her head.

"I might have called her. We still talk from time to time." His expression transformed to one of puzzlement. "Why do you ask?"

"Curiosity," she replied, innocence underscored with steel.

"I'm *happy* to answer. Tina was worried about her daughter, Maggie. We were engaged once. I'm the closest thing to a father that Maggie ever had, so when Tina was out of town and worried about her daughter, she asked me to stop by."

I clenched my fists at my sides, wishing I hadn't left my pepper spray in my car. Wishing I had it with me now. It would be worth getting in trouble to spray it right in his lying face.

He focused on my mom for the first time. "Thank God you asked, Tina. When I arrived, I found her fraternizing with this thug." He offered my mom an understanding glance, playing the scene for all it was worth. "Tina, honey, you were right. I'm sorry to tell you I caught her hanging out with this hoodlum.

CHAPTER THIRTY-FIVE

He threatened me when I asked him to leave."

I watched in disbelief as Warren spun the facts into fantasies where he reigned as the hero.

Warren glared at Kelvin. "I guess you'll know not to mess with an officer of the courts next time." He smirked and then turned to me. "And you, Maggie. Let this be a lesson to watch the company you keep and stay away from scum like—"

"Scum like what, Warren?" a melodious, powerful voice rang out from the hall.

Warren's gaze shot behind me. His eyes widened, and the sneer disappeared, replaced by his most charming smile. "Judge Thomas, how good to see you."

I turned sideways—no way was I turning my back on the slime. Suspicious of Warren's amped-up charm, my heart beat rapidly and my nails bit into my palms.

A beautiful dark skinned woman had joined us. Tall and graceful, she wore her expensive, exquisitely tailored navy skirt and jacket like armor. This was a woman who commanded any room she entered.

"Just trying to teach the youth from our community some manners. Show them the right path when apparently their parents have failed to do so," Warren continued.

"Really?" Humor and anger, an odd combination, lurked on her face. "And just what have these young people done?"

She glanced from me to Kelvin and back to Warren. Kelvin winked at me again. And the unflappable Detective Dunning bit the inside of her lip. Wicked amusement shone in her eyes as well.

"Really, Judge this is none of your concern." He frowned, respectful, but clearly annoyed that his little scene had been interrupted.

"Actually this community is always my concern, Mr. Johnson."

"Yes, well, this delinquent threatened me." He pointed at Kelvin.

"Excuse me, ma'am, that's not what happened." Kelvin shook his head.

Ma'am? Kelvin?

Judge Thomas shot daggers at Kelvin, before asking Warren in a deceptively mild voice. "Oh dear, exactly what did this young man do?"

I liked that she called Kelvin, "young man." I didn't understand what was happening here, but all of the people I trusted appeared unconcerned, even entertained, so I relaxed a little.

Until Warren opened his mouth again. "He threatened me and then later keyed my car."

Untrue! At least I thought it wasn't true. I glanced worriedly at Kelvin who responded with a look of wide-eyed innocence.

"Your lovely Porsche?" The judge tapped her chin, thoughtful.

Warren nodded.

"Oh, dear. And you saw him do this?" She frowned.

"Well, not exactly, but—"

The judge interrupted. "Officer, would you remove this young man's cuffs? Unless you fear he's going to overtake the entire squad room." Her request sounded very much like an order.

"No, ma'am." The officer squirmed with discomfort, looking to Detective Dunning for support. She nodded, and the officer continued, "I mean yes, ma'am." He fumbled with the key before successfully removing the cuffs.

Wow, this woman, this *judge* commanded respect. I added

her to my role model list: *Bad ass women.*

"If you don't mind me saying, Judge Thomas, you're taking an unusual interest in this kid." Warren's eyes narrowed.

The asshole wasn't used to things not going his way.

Judge Thomas nodded to Kelvin. "Please show me how you threatened Prosecutor Johnson."

"Yes, ma'am." His customary slouch gone, Kelvin stood with perfect posture, his tone respectful, his words carefully chosen, and his tone brimming with culture and intelligence.

What had Matt said that night at the bonfire? Something about Kelvin's wealthy upbringing and ivy league plans.

The corners of my mouth turned up. Warren had discounted Kelvin based on appearances. Watching Kelvin now, I imagined he'd make a better, more believable witness than I would.

Nice.

"This gentleman—" he nodded toward Warren "—was threatening my friend, Maggie. I simply stood by her side."

More like loomed, but I'd never tell.

"Oh, wait," Kelvin added, a frown knitting his brow.

Everyone stared at him.

He smiled. "I shook his hand and said glad to see you."

Judge Thomas pierced Warren with those awesome laser eyes. "He shook your hand?"

"Well, yes, but it was more…" He faltered.

It was past time I stepped up. "We have security cameras installed at the house." I stopped there, not wanting to be caught in a lie, but wanting Warren to believe we had him on video.

Warren's eyes narrowed for a split second, and then he put on his conciliatory, wise face. The officer who'd uncuffed Kelvin moved further away. Perhaps he'd gotten the message—if he aligned with Warren, he might as well sport a shirt that read *I'm with stupid*.

"Perhaps I've made too much of this in my desire to keep Maggie safe." He turned to Kelvin and offered his hand. "We both know what happened."

"Yes, we do." Kelvin shook his hand.

I'm pretty sure he squeezed tight, not so tight as last time, but tight enough to emphasize his point—he did indeed know the truth.

Unwilling to go down without the last word, Warren offered advice. "Well, young man, you make sure you think about how your actions can be perceived in the future. We'll let this go, this time." He turned to leave.

But Judge Thomas wasn't finished with him yet. "Mr. Johnson," she commanded in a voice like a dagger. She scrutinized Warren when he faced her, then scanned the room to include anyone else within listening distance. "Officers. *My son* had better not be dragged in again on a bogus charge. And his friends are not to be threatened in any way."

My mouth dropped open as my eyes sought Detective Dunning. She nodded, biting back a slight grin.

Freakin' unbelievably awesome. Kelvin was a bad ass judge's son. Color drained from Warren's face. This incredibly crappy day made an unexpected U-turn for the better.

"Your son? This—I—" he stuttered. "I wasn't aware you had a son."

"We downplay the relationship because of my high profile cases. And Kelvin prefers not to live in my shadow, right son?"

"Yes, Mom."

Oh boy, he was playing respectful for all it was worth.

"Well, I need to get home." Warren turned on his charming

smile, the wattage dimmer than usual. "Good night."

"Mr. Johnson." Detective Dunning stepped in his path. "One more thing." She handed him a piece of paper. "You are required by this ex parte to stay away from Maggie Bryant and Tina Bryant. If you come within one hundred yards of either of them, it will be considered a violation of this order, and you will be subject to arrest. No phone calls, no letters, no electronic communication. No visits from your *friends*." She placed a slight emphasis on the word friends.

Warren's face flushed red. "You've got to be kidding..." He surveyed the faces in the room, lingering just a second longer on me, hatred in his gaze. Then, he shrugged, attempting—and failing—to regain the upper hand. "This is all a big misunderstanding. You'll see." He spun and stalked to the exit.

Everyone stared as he shoved open the double doors and disappeared.

I wanted to shout checkmate. But the game wasn't over yet.

* * *

"He's so stupid. And arrogant. And a prick." Kelvin ranted as we waited for the elevator with our moms. He glanced at me. *And worse.*

I knew his thoughts as surely as if he'd spoken the words.

His mom skewered him with the evil eye.

"He's a prick, *ma'am*," he amended, rubbing his wrists.

Ah, this was the Kelvin I knew. Always the last word.

The judge relented with a nod. "And he's dangerous." She stared pointedly at Kelvin before turning her gaze to me. "Maggie, you are very brave. I'm glad my son has a friend like you."

Warmth spread through my chest and up into my face. Instead of blaming me for getting her son in trouble, she *approved*. Embarrassment over my response to her praise made the heat in my cheeks burn hotter.

She'd made me blush. *Good grief.* Both bad ass and kind.

I peeked at my mom to see her reaction to this praise. She smiled at me. *Wow. Unexpected.*

"You both need to be very careful." Judge Thomas reached into her purse and pulled out her card. "You call me. For anything."

I was going to need a bigger wallet if people kept handing me their cards.

"And until this is settled, you need to avoid being alone," she continued. "Call Matt or Kelvin anytime your mom's not available."

I frowned. My years of going it alone rebelled at being told what to do. I pushed the instinct aside. I had people I could count on. I swallowed. I had a bad ass judge on my side. As I tried to wrap my mind about this, my mom answered so softly I barely heard. "Thank you."

"Thank you," I echoed, but added, "I'll be okay. I can take care of myself."

Her eyes softened. She nodded. "Clearly you can." She tossed a quick raise of the brow Kelvin's way. Her *watch her* message couldn't have been clearer.

The elevator arrived.

"And don't worry about Warren's arrogance." She smiled, a dangerous flashing of teeth as we all stepped inside. "I've seen a hundred defendants like him. His arrogance will be his downfall."

When we arrived at the first floor, Judge Thomas shook our

hands. "Stay strong, Mrs. Bryant," she encouraged before she and Kelvin strode down the steps to their SUV.

Mom and I remained on the front steps, the brick building looming behind us.

"Would you like to get dinner?" she asked.

"I'm sorry I didn't tell you about the cameras," I offered.

We spoke at the same time.

"Thanks, Mom, but I'm having dinner with Matt." At least I hoped I was.

She nodded, her gaze flitting in every direction but mine. Finally, she turned sad eyes my way. "You're braver than I am, Maggie."

Uh huh. I'd known that for years. But she was reaching out to me, inviting me to talk. It was nice, I guess.

Unfortunately, the only person I wanted to spend time with right now was Matt.

Chapter Thirty-six

The truth shouldn't be so hard.
—*Maggie's Journal*

Matt wasn't at school or work or home. Yes, I'd turned into a stalker, driving around town searching for his truck.

How was I supposed to forgive him if I couldn't find him? How was he supposed to forgive me? I still didn't like that he'd made a bad situation worse; however, I'd been wrong to be so harsh—I'd taken all of my anger and inability to control the situation and directed it at him.

Not fair.

Starving, I pulled into the drive through line. While I waited, an idea occurred to me. I added an extra burger, fries, and a chocolate shake to my order, just in case I was right. A sense of certainty settled over me as I paid and headed for the lake.

Ten minutes later, I parked next to Matt's truck, grabbed dinner, and headed for the shore, using the pale moonlight to pick my way around fallen limbs. This was the place where Matt and I first made up. The place where I'd told him the truth about the abuse. Hopefully, it would be the place where we made up again. I prepared to grovel. He'd been wrong, but I'd been a jerk.

I found him sitting next to the water, hunched over, arms wrapped around his legs, chin on his knees. Misery marked his broad shoulders. He didn't hear me approach.

I stopped a few yards back, throat dry, palms damp, uncertain what to say, where to begin.

"Hey," I croaked, not how I intended the word to come out. I'd aimed for casual and friendly, and missed. His shoulders stiffened, but he didn't turn.

"Hey," he responded, so soft I strained to hear him.

Suck it up. Be brave. I crossed the final steps, stopping at his side. When he remained silent, I hesitated. He didn't move, said nothing. I bit my lip, uncertain—and a little annoyed. I plopped down beside him.

"I know I was a jerk." I plunged in. "It's just, I didn't want to mess up your perfect life. I was angry because...because..." I stopped. Telling him he was broken suddenly seemed like a bad idea.

"Because what?" His head spun toward me, frustration evident on his face. "Please don't lie."

I was prepared to lie or at least avoid the full truth, but he said please. Him and his good manners. I set the bags of food on the ground beside me and studied the patterns of moonlight on the lake. Tucking my hair behind my ear, I searched for better words.

"Maggie," he insisted after at least a minute had passed.

"Your life was perfect. You were perfect. And then you met me. Now you're in trouble at school, you quit the football team. You jeopardized your college scholarship." After a slow start, I was on a roll. "You had a great life, and now it's all messed up. You're not acting like you. I broke you." I bit out these last three words.

They shattered my heart.

Finally, I glanced at him. Eyes narrowed, he glared at me.

"Broken? You think I'm broken? Because I lost my temper for a good reason? That guy deserved to be hit." He scooped up a rock and skipped it into the lake. "I'm not freakin' broken, for God's sake. And I'm not perfect. I was never perfect."

Shocked by the anger in his voice, I stared. "But I thought you were."

He tossed another rock. "Well, that's damned unfair. I didn't ask you to put me on some…pedestal."

I felt about an inch tall. Of course he was right. It wasn't fair.

His voice softened. "There are a whole lot of options between perfect and broken."

"I know." I barely heard my whispered response.

"Do you?"

Did I? After three years of therapy, I'd better know. It's just that sometimes I failed to believe that somewhere between perfect and broken lay the elusive normal.

"I do. And I'm sorry. You're right." I held out my hand, and he took it, entwining his fingers with mine.

"I'm not sorry I quit the team. The coach was an asshole, and I took a stand." He paused. "Just like you're taking a stand." He searched my face. His intense certainty washed over me, willing me to see his side. "This is my stand."

"Okay," I whispered.

"I'm not sorry I punched Wyatt. He's an ass."

I nodded. Warren Jr., mini-ass.

Matt wasn't finished. "I'm sorry I made a scene if it made

things more uncomfortable for you."

"Okay, I get it." And I did, but I still worried. "What did your parents say?"

"They weren't happy, but they understood." He squeezed my hand. "You're invited for dinner next Sunday."

I'm certain I turned such a ghostly white my face shone like a beacon in the night.

Matt, the jerk, laughed. "They'll love you."

Eventually I had to meet his folks. I resolved to face this the way I'd faced everything else in my more broken than perfect life. One day, one step, one hurdle at a time. Besides, Matt had my back, had always had my back. I blinked back tears.

He leaned in to kiss me. "Seriously, they think you're brave." He deepened the kiss, and I loved being in his arms again.

Then my stupid stomach growled.

He rested his forehead on mine. "You going to share that food before it gets cold? I'm starving."

"Yep." Reluctantly, I slipped my hand from his and passed out the food. We ate in comfortable silence, our bodies touching from our shoulders all the way down to where my ankle rested against his calf. Our jackets kept the night wind at bay, leaving us to enjoy food, each other, and the splash of the water against the rocks.

Matt finished his burger and shoved the trash back in the bag. He sucked in a big drink of shake, slurping loudly as he drained it. "My life's not perfect." He stuck the cup in the bag.

I snorted.

"My dad's pushing me to consider East Coast colleges before I pick a school, but I like the Midwest."

I said nothing. *That was the best he had?*

"And I'm not sure how to tell him I'm thinking about not

playing football."

Okay, this surprised me.

"You're the first person I've told."

Bumping my shoulder with his, I sighed. "So he'll what…yell, take away your truck, kick you out of the house?"

He bumped me back. We both knew his dad would be disappointed but supportive.

"My mom's not a very good cook. She only makes like four meals, and they're not delicious." He lowered his voice, as if sharing a secret. "I have to eat it anyway so her feelings aren't hurt."

Waah. I refused to honor that sad story with a response. He clearly wasn't starving. Besides, now I had to eat her food on Sunday.

"Our dog chews my shoes if I don't put them away."

"Put your shoes away," I quipped.

"My grandma's taking belly dancing classes. She gave a demonstration to my friends," he moaned. "I hate it when she shimmies. I'll never get that picture out of my mind."

I chuckled. I'd like to see his grandma in action one day.

He wrapped his arm around my shoulder, and I nestled in close. He rested his chin on my head and exhaled. "That's all I got. You win. My life is pretty great."

I stared out at the lake, absorbing the soothing break of water against the rocks, examining the moon's reflection as it shimmered across the surface…thinking about that space between perfect and broken.

Matt kissed the top of my head. "I can hear your mind whirring."

Damn his ears. But this was our place. The place where we spoke the truth. So I sucked in a breath and admitted, "I'm never going to be completely normal."

He considered that for a moment. "Who really knows what normal is?" He gave me a little one-armed squeeze. "I'm never going to be perfect."

I sighed and settled in closer. If he couldn't see that he was getting the worse end of the deal, I wasn't going to worry about it. "I'll try to be normal some of the time." Throw the guy a bone.

"And I'll be perfect some of the time. Once a year. On your birthday."

We had a deal.

Chapter Thirty-seven

There are a lot of options between perfect and broken.
—Maggie's Journal

After a long decade of inactivity, the wheels of justice spun with surprising speed.

Warren was arrested within the week.

Arrested. When the news broke, my heart pounded so hard I thought it would jump from my chest. *He was arrested.* It all seemed unbelievable, like a story where justice is served and not my actual life.

People still stared at me, but the ones I cared about showed me support. It was weird, but I could handle it. Each day seemed a little easier. People knew I wasn't normal, and it bothered me less than I thought it would. After all, I'd known it all along.

And I was learning to be okay with that—with help from Doc Shirk and acceptance from Matt, who somehow seemed to like me just the way I was.

I kept the link to the article about Warren's arrest open on my phone, just to remind myself it was real.

His arraignment was scheduled for Friday afternoon. Although I wasn't needed at the hearing, the voice in my head compelled me to be there. I had to see with my own eyes that Warren Johnson, no-longer-running-for-county-prosecutor pedophile was getting what he deserved.

Justice.

Mom called the school and got me excused from sixth and seventh hour. I wasn't sure what she told them, and I didn't care.

When I pulled into the courthouse parking lot, my heart pattered. This was it. Of course, I knew there was still the trial—no way would Warren Johnson admit his guilt. But this moment when I would see him accused in a court of law…this moment was for me.

Matt had offered to bring me, but I told him to go to class. Although I read disappointment in his eyes, I knew he had a big test in Chemistry. Besides, except for the last two months, I'd been making this journey alone all of my life.

Mom had meetings and couldn't be here. She'd been unable to hide her relief at having a conflict. Frankly, I was relieved as well. We were making baby steps of progress, but her stress in the courtroom would have made me crazy.

I paused on the steps of the courthouse, my heart pounding. This intimidating stone building held my past…and I hoped that one day, maybe not today, but when this was all over, I might leave a little bit of that past behind.

Entering the building, I passed through security and headed for Courtroom J. My boots clipped along the marble floor, echoing ominously in the old building's empty hall. I felt a little woozy, disoriented, my breaths coming in and out in short gasps. I saw a restroom on my right and slipped inside.

I slammed my hands down on the counter and stared at the wild-eyed girl in the mirror. What was wrong with me?

A panic attack? Now? When justice was finally being served? Hell, no.

I curled my toes in my boots. Breathed intentionally in and out, slowing my breaths. I stared into the mirror.

"Who are you?" the girl asked.

I hesitated, waiting for familiar anger to flood through me.

"Who are you?" Her lips curled up at the corners.

I straightened and squared by shoulders. "I am Maggie Annabelle Bryant." I searched inside, but felt no frustration, no anger.

Her eyes sparkled at me.

"I am a friend…a girlfriend. I am a good student, a good athlete, a good person."

She nodded.

"I am a survivor," I said and placed my hands on my hips. I stared into her eyes. "I am a bad ass warrior."

Hell, yes. I headed back into the hall and marched to the door of Courtroom J.

When I pulled open the heavy door, a small squeak marked my entrance.

Sarah McKnight and a young man sat at one of the tables. A woman I didn't recognize, tall with highlighted blond hair wound artfully in a bun, sat at the other. Other than that, the courtroom was deserted.

I slipped into the second row behind Sarah, and she turned at the sound of me unzipping my coat. "Maggie, hi!" She left her desk and walked briskly into the spectator area to great me with a hug. "You don't need to be here."

I nodded. "I do." Running fidgety hands along my gray dress

pants, I cleared my throat. "I, uh, wasn't sure about the dress code for court." I'd chosen these pants, a white blouse, and a little black bolero jacket. And killer black boots.

"You look perfect." Her warm smile offered support, even as her razor sharp eyes revealed a core of finely honed steel. "There are more developments. He's not getting out of this."

Something eased inside me. I wouldn't want to go up against her.

She peered over my shoulder, and her smile broadened. "I'd best finish preparing."

As she returned to her desk, I glanced back. Matt strode up the aisle, dressed in khakis and a button-down shirt, his letter jacket flung over his shoulder. He was *hot*. Was this an inappropriate thought for a court of law? I checked the time. He must have left class early.

"What are you doing here?" I tried to sound accusing as he reached past me to toss his coat on top of mine.

He took my hands in his. "You're not the boss of me."

His eyes twinkled, but I read underlying concern. Should I be concerned that his butting into my business didn't bother me? In fact, my tension eased a little more with his arrival.

He'd known I needed him, despite my words. He actually was pretty darn perfect.

"I took my test over lunch." he added.

And he didn't have to be with the team because he didn't have a football game tonight.

Misreading my hesitation, he gave my hands a squeeze. "I want to be here. My folks got me excused. It's all good."

I stretched up to kiss his mouth. Just a quick peck—we were in court after all. "I'm glad you're here. Thanks."

We sat, holding hands, and watched the hands on the clock

move with slow precision toward court time. Five minutes before 3:00, I heard the creak of the heavy door opening and then the sound of footsteps. More than one person. More than two. I frowned. Footsteps and the quiet murmur of voices continued to grow.

Unable to suppress my curiosity, I glanced behind me in time to see Kelvin and Derron slip into the row behind us. They both nodded in greeting. The rows behind them filled with a mix of volleyball teammates, football players, and classmates from health class, including Mike and Elena, but no Brandi.

A weird and completely unexpected flood of emotion swamped me, because kids I was sure were fellow abuse survivors—Mike, Elena, and Derron—had shown up to support me. I was careful not to meet their eyes, uncertain what to do with this unexpected mushiness.

What were they all doing here?

Kelvin leaned forward, dressed in an actual suit and tie. Today I could totally see the resemblance to his bad ass mom. "After school field trip," he whispered, pointing at Ms. Williams as she joined Mike in the last row of students. "To support you. Mom, uh, pulled some strings with the principal. A lot of us wanted to be here." He patted my shoulder. "Had to finish class but excused from after school stuff."

Before I could even wrap my brain around the weird truth that kids who'd been whispering behind my back were now here to support me, the door opened again, and a familiar woman entered. My eyes widened. It was the woman from the restaurant. Warren's girlfriend. Ashley's mom.

She stopped in the middle of the aisle and stared at me with angry eyes, and I steeled myself for her accusations. She hadn't believed me.

Shoulders back, she marched down the aisle, stopping at our row. Close up, I could see the red, puffy eyes makeup couldn't hide. She opened her mouth to speak, then closed her trembling lips, wringing her hands. I slowly rose from my seat, heart racing.

Gathering her composure, she took my hand. "Thank you," she rasped. She dropped my hand, returned to the back of the courtroom, and took a seat halfway back in an empty row—on the prosecution's side—her face stoic.

The door opened again, drawing my attention. My once upon a time best friend swept into the courtroom like she owned the place, her black hair swung about her shoulders as she advanced. Her gorgeous dark eyes shone with determination.

Mari.

She slipped past Derron, smiling and giving my shoulder a squeeze. She leaned down to whisper, "Sorry I was out of town, but I'm here now. And I'm not going away."

Our gazes held, searching, until I nodded, "You better not."

She settled next to Kelvin and took his hand. My mouth dropped open. *Kelvin and Mari?* She winked.

Winked! Completely inappropriate for the current circumstances. My lips curved at the thought that maybe, just maybe we'd be BFFs again. I smiled at my two friends, both unexpected, both welcome.

The door at the back of the cavernous room opened, drawing everyone's attention, and a police officer escorted Warren into the courtroom. He greeted his attorney with an air kiss, nodded jovially to the officer, as if he—and everyone else—knew this was all a big mistake. He exuded smart and in-charge in his expensive navy suit, white shirt, and red power tie.

Sarah turned to me and motioned me forward. When I leaned close, she whispered, "The charges will stick. The confidence is all an act. Don't worry."

I exhaled. Placing my trust in others didn't come easily, but I was learning.

Relaxing back into the uncomfortable bench, I passed the time glaring daggers at Warren. He rubbed the back of his neck as if I'd actually nicked him. *Nice.*

Tension from Matt intruded on my carving practice, drawing my attention. If my eyes were daggers, his were big angry swords of retribution.

I elbowed him hard. "Eyes forward, McGuire," I said in my best impersonation of our principal.

He dragged his gaze from Warren to glare at me.

"Until we're out of here, I am the boss of you," I whispered, shifting my own eyes forward. It helped me to worry about him instead of the court proceedings. "No one gets to be madder than me."

Before he could respond, another door opened, and an officer of the court stepped into the room. "All rise," he commanded.

And we did.

Chapter Thirty-eight

I am more than Jane Doe 1.
—Maggie's Journal

Sarah McKnight read the charge:

"Two counts of child molestation in the first degree. Jane Doe 1 and Jane Doe 2."

Jane Doe 1. That was me. The abuse, the daily battle to do more than exist, to be more than the story of my abuse, the years spent surrounded by people yet always an island—my nightmare and battle to survive condensed into three words. Jane Doe 1.

Matt squeezed my hand, supportive, pulling me back to the moment.

Judge Hill peered over the top of his glasses, his brow marked by a heavy crease, lips turned down. "Mr. Johnson, how do you plead?"

Warren and his attorney stood. "Not guilty, Your Honor."

"Bullshit," Matt muttered under his breath.

I squeezed back, warning, don't make a scene.

Warren and his attorney remained standing. Warren appeared relaxed, confident, as if today were no more than a mere inconve-

nience. A misunderstanding. Despite the fact that he'd just been charged, he seemed just fine. Frustration clawed its way up my throat.

His attorney continued, her voice radiating confidence. "Judge Hill, we request that Mr. Johnson be released without bond. He clearly has strong ties to the community and is not a flight risk."

In a heartbeat, Sarah McKnight was back on her feet. "The prosecution strongly disagrees. We'll be filing additional charges in the coming days. We've already received a report of a third victim. Based on evidence uncovered in this investigation, police are at this moment seizing his home computer. We believe the crimes extend beyond these two cases and show a pattern of behavior."

As Sarah continued to present her case, my eyes remained fixed on Warren. Was it my imagination or did some of his confidence—his arrogance—leach from his body as she spoke?

"In addition, Mr. Johnson has already approached Jane Doe 1 and threatened her, causing us to file an ex parte order of protection. In summary, the charges are serious. Mr. Johnson faces significant prison time, and he poses a danger to the victims."

Silence filled the courtroom.

I startled when the judge finally spoke. "Bail is set at $500,000. The suspect is remanded into custody." His gavel hit the desk with a thud. "Court is dismissed."

A police officer approached Warren. "Warren Johnson, you're under arrest."

And then right there in front of me, he placed Warren in handcuffs. Handcuffs!

My heart raced, and I felt lightheaded. I never wanted to forget this moment.

Warren turned, and his eyes met mine, piercing me with hatred before shutters fell and his confident face returned.

Only this time, he wore the confidence poorly. It frayed about the edges.

The policeman turned him away from us, and they exited through a door at the side of the room.

That was it. Over an hour of waiting, twenty minutes of court, and Warren has headed for trial.

Everyone filed down the aisle and out of the courtroom. There was an awkward silence as students milled in the hallway. Ashley's mom had already disappeared. Exactly what I wanted to do.

But everyone was watching me—waiting. *Oh crap!* I shot a desperate glance at the elevators, then back at the crowd. They expected me to say something. This is why I'd have been perfectly happy to come alone.

"You did that," Matt whispered, inclining his head toward the courtroom. "You can do this." He knew I didn't like being the center of attention.

I clenched his hand tight. "Uh, thanks, everyone for being here," I mumbled.

Although I thought my words were insufficient, everyone responded at once, as if my magic words opened a floodgate of chatty kindness.

"We wanted to be here."

"You're so brave."

"It's good to see that asshole get what he deserves."

Down the hall, the elevator door opened. Kelvin and Mari waved to Matt and me before hopping inside. *Lucky.*

Some people shook my hand. One or two hugged me. Not Mike. He stood on the fringes, eyes downcast.

"Okay, everyone, let's get out of here," Ms. Williams called out.

Honest to God, I could have kissed her.

As one-by-one and two-by-two they dispersed, I scanned the crowd. The somber mood from the courtroom had transformed to normal student chaos. As if today were a regular Friday.

Then my eyes met Elena's. She stood to the side watching me. We stared at each other for a long moment, then the corners of her mouth tilted up in recognition. Maybe respect. I didn't approach her, not wanting to single her out, but I froze, unable to ignore the emotion in her eyes.

It looked like hope.

With a nod, she joined a departing pair of students.

Matt nudged me. "What's up?" He glanced between Elena and me. "I didn't know you were friends."

Shrugging, I responded, "She's nice." I wasn't going to tell her story.

She was the only one with that right.

* * *

We arrived back at school in time to tailgate. Although Matt wasn't playing, he supported the team. I could sense his restlessness during the game. He needed to be on the field.

For me, the game passed in a blur. The number of times people stopped talking when I appeared decreased drastically. Many, many, too many people nodded and smiled and *what's upped* me throughout the evening.

I'd gone from being the object of speculation and pity to being some kind of mini-celebrity. I wanted neither.

I'm not going to say this new world wasn't better than being the object of gossip and pity, but it wasn't great.

CHAPTER THIRTY-EIGHT

I swallowed hard as reality hit me.
I'd never have what I wanted most.
To be normal.

Chapter Thirty-nine

I am a reluctant, determined, scared, powerful voice.
—Maggie's Journal

The day after the arraignment, people gathered at our house, uninvited. Some of them brought food, as if we'd had a death in the family—or a birth. I suppose this exposing of the truth was a kind of rebirth.

Mom had stayed overnight with Marvin. He'd been a great support to her, and I suspected he was the reason why she'd handled everything better than I expected.

Matt and I had crashed on the couch, awakening when his friends banged on the door at 7:00 a.m., bringing boxes of donuts, jugs of milk, and travel containers of fresh, hot coffee. Kelvin and Derron high-fived me. As I slipped away to shower and change, they were telling Matt how great I was—and begging him to return to the team.

I thought, perhaps, both sentiments sounded sincere.

Mom and Marvin returned home at 8:30 with eggs, bacon, and pancake mix. Soon, delicious smells filled the crowded kitchen.

Sarah McKnight dropped by at 9:00 to tell me two additional victims had come forward. One a thirteen-year-old girl who'd been abused by Warren when she was nine, the other an eight-year-old girl. I was certain it was Ashley. Although I'd hoped he hadn't proceeded beyond grooming her for abuse, this is what I'd feared. And why I reported.

It wasn't official yet, but Sarah told me child pornography had been found on Warren's computer. It no longer mattered that I'd recanted. She said I'd started a chain of events from which Warren wouldn't escape.

Before she left, she hugged me and called me a hero.

I should have rejoiced in the victory, but instead, a bone-deep weariness settled inside me. I wasn't great, and I wasn't a hero—I'd simply had no choice.

Ms. Williams dropped by, followed by my volleyball coach and Aubree.

I fought the urge to flee outside and take down whatever BIG PARTY HERE sign had been planted in my yard.

Only there was no sign, and I'd exceeded my quota of hugs after, oh, the first two.

The doorbell rang. Again.

I stalked to the front door, determined to tell the newcomer we'd reached the maximum number of visitors allowed by city code. Flinging the door open I froze. Mari stood on the porch, holding a bouquet of flowers.

"Ohayo, tomodachi." *Good morning, friend.* She bit her bottom lip. We lunged at the same time, throwing ourselves into a big hug.

"Ohayo, tomodachi," I choked out. "Arigato." *Thank you.* Words learned in my youth flowed with ease.

We hugged for a long time—this was a hug I wanted, no,

229

needed. Tears glistened in her eyes when we broke apart. I swiped a tear from my face, and we grinned, saddened for time lost, happy for friends found.

My fault. I sobered. "I'm sorry. I—"

"Oh please, don't apologize. Aren't you going to invite me in?" She peered around me.

"You're still bossy," I retorted, pleased she hadn't changed.

"And you are the bravest person I know."

I didn't know what to say. For a moment I forgot the overcrowded house, and happiness welled inside me. My dearest friend had returned, and she thought I was brave. I took her hand and pulled her inside.

I supposed city code could accept one more.

As Mari and I arranged the flowers in a vase on the coffee table, Matt and Kelvin drifted over. Hmm, I'd have to discuss *that* relationship with Mari sometime soon.

The doorbell rang again. This time I let Derron answer—and immediately regretted it because he invited the football coach in. The coach made a beeline for Matt and me, an annoying grin on his face.

"Maggie, good job. That's the kind of courage we look for on the football field." He extended his hand.

I ignored it.

Matt stared him down until his overly large smile disappeared.

"I was wrong. I'm sorry," he apologized. It sounded sincere.

I supposed I'd be cheering for Matt during playoffs. College football or not, he wanted that State Champion ring.

The little house brimmed with laughter and chatter and the smell of good food.

It was too much.

CHAPTER THIRTY-NINE

I tried to relax and enjoy, but the frivolity of it didn't make sense to me.

"Hey," Matt whispered near my ear. "You okay?"

"Yes." Before I could stop myself, I twirled a lock of hair.

Matt raised his brow. He knew my signs. Despite my growing uneasiness, this pleased me. I clasped his hand with mine and surveyed the room. I needed to escape this mass of people who supported me—just for a while. I appreciated them, but their weird *happiness* didn't fit.

Relief, yes.

Vengeance. Some of that as well.

Satisfaction, maybe.

But the truth? I wasn't finished. Maybe I never would be. But there was something I could do. Something I needed to do.

I whispered in Matt's ear that I needed a little time alone, kissing him right there in front of the entire room to soften my words. I asked him to stay and host the impromptu party, then I fled, feeling his concerned eyes track me until I disappeared from sight.

* * *

Although it lay in the opposite direction of my intended destination, I headed for the lake first. The park stood empty, and I removed my foot from the gas, allowing the car to coast.

The lake. My first date, the place where I told Matt the truth, the place where I accepted him for who he was just as he'd accepted me. Our place.

Today the trees stood regal and barren, silhouetted with a stark beauty against the gray sky. Clustered together as though

231

even shed of their glorious fall coat, they could stand strong against stormy clouds.

I rolled down my window, braked, and closing my eyes, I let the soothing sounds of wind and water calm my thoughts. An owl hooted in a nearby tree, and my eyes flew open. It was time. I plugged an address into my phone, hit the gas, and headed north.

Fifteen minutes later, I parked my old CRV next to the curb in an upper middle class subdivision. I hadn't been back here since Mom and I moved out.

When I was eight.

I hadn't been to the house. Had, in fact, avoided this street…this neighborhood. And now, I'd finally returned for that illusive thing the doc called closure.

She'd suggested this visit, although she hadn't meant to actually come to the house. It was enough to visit in my mind.

But I wanted…needed to be here.

I turned off the ignition and sat. A couple walked past, pushing a stroller, the baby bundled in a blanket. A couple of boys rode by, laughing over some silly little boy thing, their cheeks rosy red in the chilly day.

The street emptied of activity, as if some greater force knew my intentions. I pocketed the keys and exited the car. Leaning against the passenger door, I zipped my jacket and stared across the street at the grand Victorian house on 8th Street. The house my mom had been so excited to move into with Warren.

The house where our lives were supposed to change for the better.

The house I hated so much I'd once lain awake at night and imagined burning it to the ground.

The new owners had painted it pale gray with maroon shutters. On this overcast day, it appeared gloomy and alone.

Squaring my shoulders, I stood up straight, closed my eyes, and imagined marching up the wooden porch steps.

As I neared the house, the air grew heavy and threatened to steal my breath, yet I didn't hesitate. I didn't knock or ring the bell.

I simply turned the knob, threw open the door, and swept into the entryway.

In this house was the pain.

I trod the stairs to my princess room, pausing for only a moment before I flung open this door as well.

The little girl I'd once been huddled on the bed, afraid, alone, confused. Ashamed. She stared at me, her eyes filled with knowledge no child should have.

I crossed to the bed and picked up my little self and hugged her close. "It's okay," I whispered. "I'll protect you."

I carried her down the steps.

"It's okay," I repeated. "You'll be okay. You'll be strong. You'll learn to love, to trust."

We reached the entrance. I whispered again, "You'll be okay," and kicked the door open.

With strong, sure strides, we crossed the street, never looking back.

I don't know how long I stood in silence before I felt dampness trickle down my cheeks. I thought the gray sky had finally released its rain; however, when I opened my eyes I realized it wasn't rain at all.

The sun had broken through the gray clouds. I lifted my face and allowed the warm rays to caress my wet cheeks.

I was crying.

I didn't cry for the child, but for the victory of walking her out of that house.

For showing her the love and support she'd been denied. For doing what no adult had done for me.

Say something.

Chapter Forty

I'm a little disappointed I didn't get to use my pepper spray. It would have felt soooo good to hit Warren right in the face with it.
   —Maggie's Journal

I wound through the streets back to my home where people were probably still hanging out. I hoped Matt hadn't grown tired of hosting. And it would be great if Mari were still there...and maybe even Kelvin.

Everyone else? It was nice of them to drop by, but it was fine with me if they'd already left.

I slipped my hand in my pocket. Although the police didn't think Warren would try to hurt me, the pepper spray felt good in my palm.

Warren had plenty to worry about besides me.

But still...

I thought I'd keep it. Just in case.

The End

II

Resources

Author Services and Resources

Cathy Morrison is a compelling speaker and an engaging facilitator. Learn more about her keynote speeches, author visits, and young author programs at www.cathymorrisonauthor.com.

Her website also includes helpful tip sheets for recognizing and reporting suspected abuse, as well as tips for supporting survivors of sexual abuse.

The *Say Something* **Reader's Guide** appears on the following page.

Visit www.cathymorrisonauthor.com.
Together we can make a difference.

Say Something - Readers' Guide

Maggie

- Why does Maggie talk to herself in the mirror?
- Why is it hard for Maggie to let people get close to her?
- How did Maggie feel about people showing up at her house the day after the court hearing? Why?
- How did Maggie change from the beginning of the book to the end?
- Maggie seeks both healing and justice. How are these quests similar? How are they different? Can you have one without the other?

Maggie and her mom

- How would you describe Maggie's relationship with her mom?
- How does Maggie's understanding of her mom's actions change as the book progresses?
- Should Maggie forgive her mom?

Maggie and Matt

- Why did Maggie decide to tell Matt the truth?
- Was Maggie more angry at Matt for trying to punch

Warren's nephew, Wyatt, or for quitting the football team? Was she right to be angry?
- What do you think will happen between Maggie and Matt?

Maggie and the little girl

- Why did Maggie report again for the little girl but not for herself?

Maggie and you

- Was there any part of Maggie's story you wish had been different?
- How do you feel about the idea that there's a secret club in every school?
- If you were Maggie, what would you have done?
- What do you think would be most difficult about making the call to report someone?
- How can your school make a difference? How can you make a difference?
- How can you be a friend to someone who is abused?

Literary musings

- How does the book create tension without giving graphic details?
- What artifacts does the author use and why?

Author's Note

The real Jackson County Prosecutor at the time this book was written is Jean Peters Baker. She works tirelessly on behalf of children alongside the many men and women who face the soul wearying job of tracking down and prosecuting child molesters and child pornographers. It's a difficult job, and we owe them all a debt of gratitude.

I want to thank the men and women in law enforcement who helped and inspired me. Former County Prosecutor Alison Dunning, Detective Kim Shirley-Williams and Detective Maggie McGuire.

Special thanks to Kim Shirk, licensed therapist for helping me understand the counseling process and EMDR. I could not have written this without you.

If you or someone you know is being or has been abused, there are resources for you.

There are hotlines in each state. Just search *Report Child Sexual Abuse in (your state)*. You can also call the National Center for Missing and Exploited children's CyberTipline at 800-843-5678.

1 in 4 girls, and 1 in 6 boys will be sexually abused by the age of 18. For more information about child sexual abuse, visit www.MOCSA.org or your local support organization. MOCSA provides services in the Kansas City area, but they also have helpful information and resources online.

I also have helpful tip sheets on my website www.cathymor-risonauthor.com.

Prevent child sexual abuse. *Say something.*

Made in the USA
Lexington, KY
24 October 2019